RAVAGERS 2

C.A. GLEASON

Cover art by Darko Tomic

ISBN: 9798840865729

PART 1

Planet Adelpa

CHAPTER 1

The Adelpa HJC, a hybrid jet/helicopter—A-brid for short—was in hover mode after the pilot transformed it into a helicopter.

That was after first jetting to the set coordinates at Corbin Mero's command to give him time. He knew that if there were any predators in the territory, they were locked on the aircraft and not himself.

But he had only minutes until everything changed, if that. Probably only seconds.

In a way, he was counting on being hunted because he forced himself to think like a fellow predator, and the part of him that was human relied on plan A going to hell; thus he had a backup plan, and even backup plans.

He grabbed the black rope and placed both of his gloved hands, applying the appropriate pressure, giving it a tug to be sure, eyeing the forever of mist stretching beneath his boots.

A Rovla sniper rifle strapped and pressing across his back, side arm securely fastened on his hip, he was ready. But he had learned that the battles against the beasts sometimes came down to a knife.

That was why he also had a tactical knife. It was strapped to his waist opposite the pistol. He could and would wield the knife—and quickly—if all of his weapons that fired bullets either jammed or clicked empty.

Running low on ammo would take a while considering how many loaded magazines he had stuffed into his LBV (load bearing vest).

He briefly wondered if the camo paint he'd added to his face would aid in his camouflage or if they were as close as he suspected they might be. If they were, they'd have sniffed out the A-brid before it arrived, and heard it even before then.

Being aware of their locations—he'd seen the heat maps—was essential to remaining alive, and there seemed to always be stragglers, singles away from the main packs. Scouts, just as he was.

It was possible that there were scouts that weren't deterred by the noisy aircraft and were hunting him. It was risky being on the planet at all, but in order to achieve what he wanted, risking his life was necessary.

He gave the pilot a thumbs up and again squeezed the rope with both gloved hands, draping his right leg over the length of the rope with his left leg behind it, and slid down, dropping through the mist toward ground most would consider to be a death sentence.

The pillowy mist got thicker the further down he descended, but he'd scouted the location days before, and knew precisely where he was going to touch down with his tightly-laced, booted feet.

The pilot had flown him over the landscape, and multiple times, giving Mero the time to decide on the perfect spot.

He'd also faked dummy landings to throw them off in case they planned to ambush him. It was possible they could be at every one of them, but it wasn't likely, and they couldn't know which location he'd actually chosen.

At least he hoped not.

The location he had chosen was flat and slightly elevated, just in case he inadvertently fell into a trap.

Mero wouldn't put any strategies past them, and he would assume they'd done the same as him—prepared—and were as ready for him as he was for them, wherever he landed.

But if they were positioned at multiple locations at once, that would be less he would face when he put his boots on the ground, and he was confident in his weapons as long as they were loaded.

It was a risk to fly over the planet at all, as he'd been warned, but he was willing to take the risk because of what was at stake.

Even though the Ravagers had been known to destroy aircraft

while in flight, the last time that happened was during the mission ten years ago. Much more had been learned about the enemy since then.

Still, mountains and hills hadn't gone anywhere, or changed that could be seen in those ten years, not to human eyes. Often the slopes of the mountains were layered terrain, almost like stories of a giant building, but one shaped as craggy steps.

Steps that beasts could use as a leaping off point to spring an attack.

Glancing upward, the A-brid continued to fall away, and peering back down trees rose up, and the alien leaves looked poisonous to the touch. Especially if consumed by mistake as the result of starvation, a fate which had befallen colonists.

To be safe, and consistent, he would view everything in sight as a threat or an enemy until Enginsan Adelpa was satisfied, and Enginsan being satisfied meant the surface was decimated, the creatures exterminated, and then Mero would get what he desired.

Scouting artillery and missile targets that would begin decimating their population—because of their ability for subterfuge—was why he was there. Mero was the only man Enginsan trusted to get the job done to his satisfaction.

Mero getting the job done to Enginsan's satisfaction meant a dramatic increase to his bank account and also some impressive perks.

The only thing—things—in his way were the beasts and he'd made up his mind about their fate when Enginsan first pitched him the plan.

At first, it sounded like a suicide mission, but one that seemed less so the more Enginsan explained what the end result would be.

Might be.

Touching down on the final location, he tugged on the rope and it snaked upward into the impenetrable white mist above him, lassoing out of view before disappearing altogether, and now hidden except to the personnel on board.

Then he heard the aircraft thunder away. He turned in a circle, scanning for any movement.

There was none.

Mero was on his own.

He pushed the shoulder mic on his radio. "Base, this is Mero. Radio check."

"Good check, Mero."

Lucky for them there was an immediate response. If there wasn't, he would have fired anyone manning the radio.

Any RTO (radio transmitter operator) understood the consequence of violating his standard because he'd warned them all.

And there were too many RTOs. It was a test of who was reliable, and if they were, how committed. What was going on was no longer a military operation, and civilians were unpredictable, prior service or not.

What worked best for him was to work with personnel who could keep up with his standard, which was rare. Ryke being one of the few exceptions. And Enginsan of course. The rest he would have trusted were dead. And they'd died here.

He'd waited long enough. Still, Mero slowly slid the sniper rifle across his body and held it at the ready.

There was no scope attached. A scope wasn't necessary at the range he would fire the high-caliber weapon if one of them stalked him, but there was a scope in a cargo pocket in case he decided it was needed.

There was a silencer attached at the end of the barrel. He understood that the enemy would even hear a round fired from a silenced weapon, but he would likely encounter only rogue scouts.

Outliers would have trouble identifying his position before backup could arrive. Especially if he fired the weapon only once, and for Mero it was typically one shot, one kill.

Firing his sniper rifle twice would likely mean avoiding jaws and claws, but he was confident enough in his ability as a marksman to prevent that.

During an operation like this one, if he needed to fire his weapon three times, he was a dead man.

If everything went south and he needed to be picked back up again sooner than planned, then it would be by the same A-brid that had dropped him off, and it would land out in the open at a predetermined location Mero had designated, halfway to Plan A.

But that would only happen if he needed to contact base if everything went very wrong. And if he absolutely needed to, he could take advantage of the big guns; Adelpa 3 fighter jets, and all of their firepower.

Mero wouldn't make the mistakes of others who'd set foot on this planet, who didn't have all of the knowledge he did, and also couldn't have been able to command Enginsan's personal arsenal with the push of a button and a voice command.

The terrain was ideal for what was planned for Nev, but that would be after the artillery strikes. There were always stragglers. When it came to those beasts, there always were rogues.

Although Mero didn't know Nev personally, he didn't give a lick about what Enginsan wanted done to him.

The former captain was the reason Enginsan didn't have control over the planet yet, and why Mero didn't have a resort to himself already. And that meant delaying impressing the women Mero dated. He was anxious for a poke at a resort that he owned.

The light mist ahead shifted, something scrambling. Once again, there was nothing but silence.

He'd studied their behavior on the ground—as he was now—and also by air, but also studied the research of others, and from everyone involved during previous missions, so he knew that silence was deceptive. They could be loud or quiet.

It was heading for the ridge and Mero aimed through the iron sights of the sniper rifle. He squeezed the trigger and sniped the Ravager scout in the ear.

It collapsed onto the rock outcropping. Mero had expected more of them. Well, he was sure there were more, but they'd yet to reveal themselves.

Its carcass would soon be discovered by others of its kind and buried; no doubt they were nearby and incoming, so he needed to hustle.

Mero had marked the targeting locations by sending coordinates. The digital terrain marker was no bigger than a small flashlight. He had a flashlight too in case everything went south and the buzz of night arrived before he could get back to base.

The large packs of predators would be decimated shortly after his boots left the ground. He'd also identified the perfect spot to dump Nev—formerly *Captain Nev*—after the initial phase of the new plan.

Nev's history meant that he wasn't a man to be taken lightly, but he would be facing beasts, and sooner or later he'd be torn apart. And within seconds, it only took one.

"Base, this is Mero."

"Go ahead, Mero."

"We're good to go."

Everything was set up perfectly. Enginsan's wealth would gain him the planet and get him revenge against Nev, and Mero would be richer and own a resort with a spectacular view, having earned it.

And there were so many locations to choose from. He could retire as a military contractor, entertain guests, and enjoy a view for the rest of his life, and he planned on living a long time.

He'd scouted several locations where his resort would be built with the stipulation—in writing, and signed by Enginsan—that it would remain in his family and also, it would not be constructed near any bombardments by artillery shells and missiles.

Past, present, or future, he desired unscorched ground. His biggest problem was deciding on which view.

He wondered if his father, or even grandfather, Corbin Mero I, would have been proud of his accomplishments if they were still alive.

If everything worked out according to plan, Mero suspected his father would have indeed been proud of him, based on the continuance of the Mero legacy.

"Are you requesting an early pickup?"

"Negative. I'll hump it to the A-brid. Plan A location, break . . . Tell those soft civilians comfortable behind the controls of pristine destructive weaponry in a climate controlled environment to be ready. Tell them to kill anything that moves within the terrain I've designated after I've returned. But *after I've returned,* and *not* before. I want to see mushroom clouds."

"Understood."

A familiar headache. Mero needed a coffee. It was best to enjoy a coffee from orbit.

"Never mind. I'll tell them myself."

CHAPTER 2

Mero was unnoticed. He practically watched his investments slipping away. Because of their actions.

Are you here to fuck or fight?

He thought about saying it aloud, or some variation, but didn't. Not yet. That would have been the same mistake he'd learned as a youngster, when his father taught him the ways of the hunt, and that the first impulse was typically wrong.

Weakness was something predators wanted to pounce, but unless that could be done the first time, and the result a kill, it was best to make sure the prey was at its weakest to ensure success.

There were too many of all of them. Enough to collectively turn against him, no matter how much power and control he wielded, so he waited for the appropriate opportunity.

Instead of doing what he initially wanted to do, which was chew out anyone within the sound of his voice, all of them at the same time if need be, he judged what was before him as accurately as anyone else might view it.

Beautiful women who had no place here other than for pleasure of those who saw fit to manipulate the standards with select paperwork to bring them here, in his opinion. Not that he minded ogling either.

Their other qualifications were top notch though. He was as sure of that too. All of them were, the men and the women, but he wouldn't have chosen the men either.

Judging by their behavior, he was practically watching a bar, and one without alcohol being served, but he suspected it was hidden nearby, no doubt waiting to be drunk in rooms after shifts were over.

Although there were some relationships forming—when men and women were together there was no alternative—he would apply his skills at hunting to identify the weakness of each relationship and make one of the women his own for the time that he wanted.

He would ensure that the man interested in her the way all men were interested in women would be notified of how Mero had taken her away for his pleasure, explained in detail—anonymously—about the trophy who was now his to take on the balcony of the resort in his mind.

His personal resort that would be built to his standards.

His eyes continued to hunt, to identify weaknesses he could exploit, but he'd yet to walk forward, so still he'd yet to be seen, which only proved how preoccupied they all were with courting. It was the wrong direction.

Although Enginsan had accomplished much, his arrogance left boot laces untied that needed to be retied and cinched tightly. Enginsan believed that his wealth and power would gain him the planet.

Eventually. No matter what. No matter the cost.

Mero knew differently, and perhaps Enginsan knew it too on a certain level, and that was likely why Mero had been brought on board.

The truth was that all great feats were accomplished using the most primitive of skills, and with Mero came those skills, making him the perfect tool, or even weapon to wield, in order for Enginsan to gain the planet he desired.

Hunting, strength in numbers, hiring weaknesses, overkill, overconfidence, Mero was all of those traits contained within one person. He was someone capable of capping every fearable outcome to accomplish a main goal.

Mero understood his role as one of many and aside from being a weapon, he could fill gaps, raise unevenness, and plug leaks.

He often seemed as any of them before they truly knew him. Not that he allowed anyone to know him fully, only what he was capable of in his viciousness of action during the temporary parameters of a given situation.

He was a predator who preyed on prey and predator alike. But sometimes, the best hunters disguised themselves as the prey they would take down and ravage. It was a lesson learned during his past that he would apply now and also in the future.

Disguising himself would no longer take place here. He'd already decided, his impatience wearing through.

Here, he would reveal himself as any predator to prey when giving chase, as he no longer cared about the outcome, or how he was perceived.

Not to those who would not remain, and would not remain after the planet was under control.

Mero drank down the last of the coffee, the sludgy drippings that had been in the pot, ignoring the burning, and threw the mug with adjustable heat across the room.

It skidded across the floor before shattering against the wall, ending all conversations, allowing himself to finally be noticed, and they reacted as if a Ravager had gotten on board.

He took pleasure in seeing his ferocity reflected on expressions, even those with battle experience. Even soldiers who were no longer soldiers could be vulnerable when courting.

But not all of them had been real soldiers. Some of them had only pretended to be soldiers. Even though they'd worn a uniform and carried a weapon, they'd merely weathered a storm.

Even Enginsan understood that humans were often the best bait for what they faced on the surface of the planet below them, especially after Mero had reiterated that fact.

"Let's play a game. If someone can explain their value to what we are doing to my satisfaction, they'll remain here, on board. If not, you go to the base on the surface."

He intended on sending them all to the surface base save a few. The game was his alone—they would experience no winning or even joy from it—as he searched for the first of his many prey for the evening.

Chewing out underlings always allowed him to sleep better, and the man he finally decided on was feigning confidence, staring right at him, but he couldn't trick Mero.

"I'll start with you."

Weakness glimmered like a passing shadow, before the man's confidence—faked confidence—returned, and Mero stepped toward the first pounce.

FOUR MONTHS LATER

CHAPTER 3

Ryke flicked the cigarette butt. Smoked to a nub, its glow was sucked out, propelled by the rotating blades and vociferous whir of the A-brid.

It had been months since the planet was hit with artillery strikes, airstrikes, and even Mero gas, but the animals still lived. No one knew how that was possible, which meant resuming ground patrol operations.

Once they returned, they would fall in with the rest of them. But that would be after their little hush hush side mission was accomplished.

The A-brid could maintain the current elevation or it could transform into a jet if required, something Ryke had dared the pilot to do, out of boredom.

But that transformation would require landing, the pilot had informed him, and landing at the moment would be unwise.

"I think you started a forest fire," Kilroy said.

Ryke glared. "Who cares?"

Kilroy gave Ryke a look like maybe he should. But then changed his mind. "I suppose it doesn't matter. I heard the bombings are going to resume anyway."

"Not that they do any good. Still, I heard Enginsan's going to hit the planet with a ton of more missiles."

"So."

Ryke shrugged. "What do you know?"

"I heard he might drop nukes."

"And damage his precious planet? No way."

"You think so?"

Ryke nodded.

"Good."

"No matter what the real plan is, *they* won't be alive much longer. We can do whatever we want."

"I can't believe just one of them can take down an aircraft. I mean how in the hell is that possible?"

"Whenever there's an egress, there's always an ingress."

"I guess. Look at that one."

"Stupid animals. Won't stop following us."

Ravagers galloped beneath the aircraft, trying to keep up with it from the ground, craning their striped heads to look upward. No doubt they were aggravated by the barrages of ordnance and hadn't forgotten.

Those that couldn't keep up fell behind but there were thousands more to take their place, so it seemed they were constant. And that was only directly beneath them. Who knew how many of them there were.

The A-brid flew directly over a heavily populated territory, and the Ravagers clearly understood the aircraft was a threat. Perhaps some of them had even seen an A-brid flying ten years ago.

"Pass it over."

Ryke's fellow merc disengaged the weapon from the gun rack and hefted it over to him, nearly dropping it.

"You drop my weapon, I'll throw you out."

Kilroy grinned. "Fuck off."

Smirking, Ryke grabbed hold of the powerful, single-shot bolt-action Rovla sniper rifle, settling it comfortably over his lap, took aim, and fired.

He fired again, and again, and again, each pull of the trigger sending a bullet just above the neck, and each bullet catapulting a one-ton quadruped—more or less—into a death throe.

That didn't deter Ravagers from continuing to stalk what flew above them, but others did rush to sniff the dead ones, or use their jaws to pull them away until they were out of sight, causing slight concern on the faces of the airborne mercenaries above.

"What do you think they do with their wounded?"

"The way I shoot? Dead you mean."

"Fine, what the hell do you think they do with the dead?"

"I don't care. I can shoot forty out of forty but I still miss the bowl when I piss. Explain that one to me."

"Maybe you should just go outside like I do. Especially while we're here."

"And get my boys bitten off? No thanks."

Rob heard voices before the gunshots, but because he had no idea where he was or what was going on—as he was coming to—he felt like he was dreaming, and having the initial panic of a nightmare.

Every planet had a different feel, as obvious as experiencing different seasons whenever the weather changed. Rob and his wife, Kate, had even visited Earth since his retirement, something he'd always wanted to do but especially with her alongside him.

As his mind sharpened, somehow he knew he was back on Planet Tuhrelevim. He recognized the smells and felt the humidity, the familiarity of everything about it, including the faint scent of its inhabitants, even while airborne.

The scent of them dominated, which made sense because Ravagers dominated the planet alongside Maulers. It seemed that hadn't changed since he'd last been there.

Rob also detected faint traces of ordnance. There'd been bombings, recent ones, and the unmistakable fuel-like odor that had not only destroyed but also burned.

A foul smell to civilians, but ironically, to someone like him, the bombings reminded him of the feeling of home, similar to the sound of gunfire, and also wherever it was that a soldier was stationed but returning after a mission.

That included a dangerous planet teeming with wild, intelligent, and cunning predators like Tuhrelevim.

Rob knew he'd been drugged but its effect lessened as the seconds ticked by. Unfortunately, he was forced to listen to their boyish conversation. Rantings by Ryke and Kilroy, men who'd been in the military, but no longer were.

They were former soldiers who hadn't seen enough war to halt their desire to kill for sport, for fun, or even for target practice, especially the one called Ryke.

Rob had seen enough of their brutality. He no longer felt completely groggy. He felt more and more lucid with every waking moment but they hadn't remarked that he was conscious.

Except he *was* waking up, so that part had been planned.

They, whoever *they* were, probably wanted him dead, but *they* hadn't killed him yet. His wonderings of why he was there and where they were taking him would soon be answered.

And then he noted something else while aboard the A-brid, thundering over ground clawed by paws galloping beneath, its familiar shadow giving him the confidence to finally antagonize them.

It was a life raft that might get him out of the mess, and that would be aided by unbound hands. That in itself was a mystery.

Did they not know who he was? Had they not heard about all that he'd been through and what he was capable of?

Impossible.

The fact that he was even there meant that they did. But why all of the subterfuge?

CHAPTER 4

Ryke had resumed shooting. By the reaction of Kilroy, the man next to him, Ryke's shots were kills. Gunshot after gunshot after gunshot from the sniper rifle was finally interrupted by Rob's voice.

"They're not going to like that. You guys should have chain guns."

"They're just stupid animals, it doesn't matter," Ryke said without turning, as if he'd been waiting. "They don't think!"

"They're not stupid, you fucking coward. You might as well find a giant blender, turn it on, and jump in. You're going to end up a bloody mess with that attitude."

That got Ryke's attention. That twisted his view. Accompanied by a confident smirk.

"They're selfless. They'll sacrifice themselves. And before you know it, one will appear out of nowhere, casting you in shadow, and before you can pull the trigger."

It was as if the rotating blades keeping them airborne suddenly froze in place, and the only sound was the powerful wind from the flight. All attention had turned toward Rob, and any hint of humor vanished.

"Coming from Captain—sorry—*former* Captain Nev," Ryke said, "responsible for killing . . . how many thousands of them?"

Rob hadn't thought of himself as a captain for quite some time. Nor had he been called Nev. His first name was Robert but he preferred Rob these days. Sometimes Kate called him Robert Henry Nev when he was in hot water with her.

"He was armed with Shoulder Devils, so were his accomplices," Kilroy said. "Who knows. Uncountable. He thought he was a one man army."

Nev would not think of himself as Rob again until he was off planet.

Accomplices? It was totally different when they were doing what they were doing—it was a mission—and he wanted to tell them, explain that fact with an edge only a former officer was capable of.

But he was still getting his bearings. He should wait until his strength could back up his words.

"He doesn't remember us, look at him. Still all doped up. That drink did its job. But you had a contingency plan for that sort of thing, didn't you? Your bitch wife got away, otherwise she'd be here with you."

Nev and Kate did indeed have a plan in case their lives after the mission went awry, including expediting his retirement. Transportation to a secret location guarded with military contingencies, paid with a savings account that Nev had earned while serving.

They had understood the danger they were in and likely would be in until the end of their lives. As long as Enginsan Adelpa himself was alive, then they were within his wealthy reach.

Enginsan Borovich Adelpa; inventor, ruthless business man, egomaniac, and zillionaire.

Nev must have fallen unconscious before the plan was fully implemented, but it had succeeded to his satisfaction because Kate wasn't there alongside him as they'd threatened. She'd gotten away.

The fact that they were bitter about it gave him hope she was where he envisioned they'd be safest as man and wife. And he hoped to join her soon.

However they had located them, he would discover, but whatever they'd used to knock him out was still affecting him. He wasn't one hundred percent.

Still, he was going to kill Ryke for talking about his wife that way. Whoever he really was, besides being ex-military, he was a stooge for Enginsan.

Nev had never met Enginsan but his reputation as an inventor and weapons dealer preceded him. He'd also heard some disturbing rumors, and if Nev were still a betting man, he would bet that those rumors were true.

Enginsan, in all likelihood, plotted murders, was used to getting whatever he wanted, and—Nev learned firsthand over the years since leaving the planet but especially now—was an uncompromising son of a bitch.

"What the hell are you people doing on Tuhrelevim anyway?"

"You're here too, fucker. And it ain't called Tuhrelevim anymore, dumb ass."

Of the two, Ryke is in charge.

"How did you find me?"

"Does it matter? You're here. And you're never leaving."

"Let me guess, it's called Planet Adelpa now."

"Affirmative. I guess you're not as dumb as you look."

Nev wanted to throat punch Ryke for being such an asshole, and also do worse, and also do the same to everyone else involved in bringing him back to the planet.

"I told Enginsan that we should just shoot you. But this is what he wants."

"To take me sightseeing?"

"No smartass. To get eaten."

"Smartass? I'm your elder by almost twenty years by the look of you. Show some respect."

"Nope. You're our prisoner."

Nev leaned, slightly and undetected, glancing below, seeing what he thought he would; determined striped hunters, the beasts he knew very well having battled so many of them.

Ryke slid the sniper rifle to Kilroy, who placed the weapon on the gun rack, shuffled his feet and faced Nev, glancing down at Nev's unbound hands. "What are you going to do about it, old man?"

CHAPTER 5

Nev's hands had been left unbound on purpose. Ryke wanted the fight. And he wanted to fight Nev even though he'd heard of him and what he'd done in the past.

But there were few who truly knew how much of a threat Nev was, and it wasn't anyone in their twenties.

Men like Ryke practically believed they were invincible, and Nev remembered feeling the same way when he was their age, but someone like Sergeant Major Kayner could have kicked his ass.

And if Nimbus, Horne, or Makada were still alive, there wouldn't have been such a dramatic production to get revenge; Nev would be dead.

It seemed his abductors really meant to kill him, but if they were smart, they would have just put a bullet in his head before he was ever brought back to the planet, as Ryke had apparently suggested to Enginsan, not follow through with such an elaborate scheme.

It wasn't as if Nev didn't make mistakes; he'd confused the hierarchy between Ravagers and Maulers upon first sight of a Mauler, but Enginsan's biggest error was overlooking the fact that someone like Nev wasn't a typical loose end.

Nev was battle hardened with decades of military experience under his belt, and that also included battling beasts. Nev was the type of loose end that could transform from ally to enemy and only a spoiled and rich civilian could miss it.

What was the difference between a man in his twenties and a man in his forties who was the same size and had the same training?

Experience.

And if they were both fighters, then the man in his forties likely had fought more times.

Kilroy was a stooge, but Ryke was a familiar sort. Nev had encountered people like him before. Knew them well too, but Ryke wasn't as carefully composed as someone like Major Makada had been. Difficult to push a man like that. To manipulate him.

Especially when he didn't want to be pushed. Not with all of those years of service and doing the same pushing to soldiers who were of lower rank. It was very difficult to rattle military bearing that had been rock solid for decades.

Ryke hadn't lived long enough to compare, or even implement the strengths of being a soldier for very long. He was far too young. And he was unimpressive aside from his arrogance and physicality.

Ryke looked strong though. No doubt he did physical training daily. Because of all of Nev's experience, he understood not to underestimate any enemy, no matter what they looked like, or how much he wanted to punch him in the face.

No longer wearing rank because he was a mercenary, the merc called Ryke had a short, ugly beard. Unregulated even for an ex-soldier in Nev's personal opinion. Defiant in its length. Being prior service meant Ryke was a risk taker.

Definitely partly or mostly crazy judging by the look in his eyes, and that gave Nev the sense that Ryke could make a mistake.

Could be pushed into making a mistake. One that could benefit a man like himself in such a situation.

His buddy, Kilroy, who'd been chatting with him earlier, was equally muscular but even more unimpressive.

Nev spread his hands and clenched them into fists. "I've fought plenty tougher than you, kid."

Nev gauged Ryke's reaction, whose confidence faltered but only momentarily. Then his humor returned. Ryke didn't believe Nev, or at least didn't believe he could handle the throttling he planned on giving him.

Maybe he was right.

Again, Nev thought back to Major Makada, their brutal fight, and Nev had only survived because of the unexpected. If that

Mauler hadn't come along . . .

"You sure you want to do this?"

Nev's answer was Ryke whistling to the pilot and then the A-brid descending, the ground still a blur but gradually rising toward them. He meant to throw him out. But he would need Kilroy's help.

Nev stood, fists clenched.

Ryke stood as well. "This fucker thinks he's going to do what he did before."

"You're damn right I will."

Kilroy remained seated but a hard look by Ryke shot him up. "We should rush him."

The mercs hesitated. They clearly didn't want to fight him that way, together, but also neither of them wanted to go first.

Ryke went for a throat punch, but Nev's forearm glanced the blow, and hunched, Nev rammed into him with his shoulder, even though he really wanted to punch Ryke in the face, bloody his nose, and water his eyes.

Instead of doing what would have been most satisfying, Nev went for the body with everything he had instead, his right hand sending endless hooks thudding against Ryke's ribcage. Nev heard splintering like dried wood.

Ryke should have been wearing armor when facing someone such as him, but Nev was sure Ryke wanted to stay loose for the fight he'd planned, and knowing that had allowed Nev to capitalize on the younger man's mistake.

Even though Nev was confident in his hand to hand skills, he wasn't surprised when the fight didn't go as he planned, and he was grabbed from behind by Kilroy.

Ryke's accomplice was attempting to squeeze the life out of him, so Nev reached down and lifted open a toolbox next to his knee, grabbed a laser torch, ignited its hot white fire, and held the heat against interlocked hands across his chest.

Since Ryke was in pain and stunned from the body blows, Nev easily broke out of Kilroy's grasp as he shrieked from being burned. He also dropped a stun gun.

Nev turned and raised a boot and kicked downward, stomping on Kilroy's knee, feeling it give and hearing it tear. The confirmation of the injury was the man yelling differently than being burned and clutching his knee with scorched hands.

An eye jab allowed Nev to rip away the Rovla assault rifle Kilroy had armed himself with before the kick, and Nev flipped the weapon and used it to crush his nose with a butt stroke.

Before blood could flow out of Kilroy's nose or his eyes could clear from instant tears, Nev righted the weapon and pulled the trigger. The burst of bullets misshaped his face and dropped him.

When Ryke grimaced and made an awkward lunge, Nev, out of the corner of his eye, saw, quickly aimed and shot him too, also with a controlled burst, the reverberation of the automatic gunfire deafening within such a small space.

As Ryke fell, Nev saw shock in his eyes.

Nev didn't want to shoot the pilot, for obvious reasons, but the pilot was not so sneakily reaching for a pistol holstered on his hip.

He'd nearly unbuckled the clasp, making his intent clear, so Nev disintegrated the shaded visor attached to his helmet, causing him to slump.

The A-brid plummeted, and Nev dropped the Rovla, the rifle skittering across the floor out of reach before falling out into the blur.

"Shit!"

Quickly, Nev climbed down into the hover skiff attached to the belly of the A-brid, ignoring the initials of *EBA* that were there, and started up the controls, the ground rising at a dizzying rush.

Nev pulled the attachment lever and accelerated to full speed, touching down with momentum, embracing another feeling of familiarity, similar to riding a bike later in life having ridden one as a boy.

Without turning, as he was positive the beasts had sighted the skiff with a human driving it, he spied a rocky valley hollowed out and steered toward it, twisting the throttle to full speed, over one hundred miles per hour.

The A-brid crashed to the ground and exploded.

He twisted his view, keeping an eye on the advancing enemy. Fortunately the rushing mass of them had fallen behind, distracted by the burning aircraft, but still he'd been seen, which meant he would be hunted.

Nev regarded the dark mountains in the distance, looming. Once again, he felt the peculiar familiarity of home.

CHAPTER 6

Enginsan's wife had been missing for five years. He did indeed miss her—missed who she was before turning against him—but it was after the argument at one of his many restaurants—that only the elite could afford—when he'd decided there was no turning back.

There'd been such an embarrassing shouting match; it was the only thing he couldn't control with his wealth. Both of them having too many drinks was why it happened, but when she'd gone to the restroom, it was enough time for his head to clear and make a decision.

She wasn't seen coming out of the restroom. And she never made it back to the table. In fact, she was never seen again.

He'd made the mistake of marrying someone who loved animals, and although that had been attractive to him at first, of course his wife hated what happened on the planet. His involvement bled out over the news for years, as well as his wife's opinion that Ravagers were highly intelligent, had families, and were "like us."

Their final argument at the restaurant had been about her objection to him resuming his takeover of the planet, something she'd said was impossible, and in her opinion had been a mistake in the first place and reminiscent to some tyrannical explorers during Earth's past.

Her examples were reminiscent to those who weren't willing to go far enough in his opinion, the objections absurd, which was why he'd allowed his wife to disappear. He couldn't have someone so close speaking out against him, especially after what would have ended up as a nasty and expensive divorce.

Him owning the restaurant helped in the cover-up, but what didn't help was that there were too many disgruntled employees of his many companies. No doubt one of them witnessed enough to report suspicions and could care less how much he paid them off, or heard second hand and talked to the press.

He'd given up paying investigators to find the truth, and whomever it had been was lucky. They would have suffered the same fate as Nev, along with many others standing in his way since Operation Tuhrelevim. The Ravagers didn't even leave bones.

Because of the news and how fast news spread, the depth of Enginsan's involvement in Operation Tuhrelevim became known. Similar to how many view a god, he was ever present, pulling the strings, and the one who was really in charge.

He'd wanted to keep all of that a secret, but that was difficult when his name was on the vehicles and aircraft. He'd learned from the mistake and created a fictional name for his line of guns, naming them Rovla.

Even after hiding evidence, somehow people still suspected the truth. Except he was smart enough to know when to allow those who were good at something to do what they were best at and only step in if he had to, with the understanding that the greatest feats often took more time than planned.

Sometimes years, decades, or even centuries.

Not that he was really hiding anything at this point, having named the planet after himself, but any illegal activity requested on his behalf would be extremely difficult to prove, if not impossible.

There was a long list of people who would be imprisoned long before himself, them acting as a buffer. But so far no one had gone to prison, and many who were perceived as guilty were dead.

And also, this was outer space.

Difficult to prosecute someone out among the stars, especially without proof and based on speculation and hearsay. The events happened a long time ago and lately it was full steam ahead.

By trusting those he'd entrusted, allowing them to fulfill their roles, it allowed him to learn from their mistakes.

Once he was integrally involved by being located in orbit, Enginsan hadn't made the same mistakes as Colonel Horne. He had an abundance of firepower at his disposal and also deployed plenty of expendable mercenaries.

Men and women who would cross the line far easier than trained, disciplined soldiers who were loyal to ideals.

Of all of them, Enginsan had two elite guards; Ryke and Mero. But Ryke's whereabouts were currently unknown. It had been reported that he'd disappeared after lifting off with the treacherous —but unconscious—Nev.

If Enginsan were to judge Mero's personality type, he would say that he was former Captain Nev's mild mannered equivalent.

Both Ryke and Mero were prior service but Mero differentiated himself from Nev in that he understood what Planet Adelpa—formerly Planet Tuhrelevim—had to offer. And Mero often reminded Enginsan of what he'd been promised.

Unfortunately with strength came entitlement in Mero's case, because Mero was Corbin Mero's grandson. Corbin Mero had been the inventor of Mero gas and an associate of Enginsan's own father.

Corbin Mero III was born into wealth, and because of that, Enginsan thought he was born insecure. Most who inherited were, but to Mero's credit, and why Enginsan hired him, was that he wanted to make his own way.

Mero overcompensated by being proficient at weapons handling, hand to hand combat, hunting, and other unnecessary skills as well as being so rich, which he liked to brag about, bringing them up nonchalantly while using non sequiturs.

Mero was overly confident, and quite arrogant, evident by the constant smirk on his face. Enginsan found him grating personally, but Mero would prove useful if the planet could finally be under his control.

Hopefully, Ryke and Kilroy had been successful at dumping the traitor. Hopefully, Nev was dead. Enginsan didn't really care if Ryke and Kilroy were dead too. There would be no rescue. That way, he could deny it ever happened.

Ryke and Kilroy had been trusted to get it done. But them being still alive or not was irrelevant; all Enginsan really wanted was for Nev to be thrown out of an A-brid, realizing his mistakes before being overwhelmed like so many others.

Enemies of his who'd disappeared from the universe without a trace. Not even their bones would be found.

The benefit of Ryke still being alive was that Enginsan could maintain extra control over Mero. Mero seemed undisciplined without Ryke around. They'd served together and their friendship distracted Mero from being overtly difficult.

For some reason, Mero listened to Ryke, which made him somewhat controllable. Whenever he wasn't out hunting, which was seldom.

Regardless of Mero's birthright, and needing to practically be pampered, he was a reliable asset and well-trained.

The elevator opened.

CHAPTER 7

Spying the alluring glint and shine of his armaments, some so polished that Enginsan observed a distorted reflection of himself, they made him look as large as he felt.

His creations were the children he'd never had but loved just as much, and loved showing them off to anyone even more, or marveling about them when he was alone.

The promise of their destructive power made him proud.

He could have easily sent more weapons along with Horne, and even transported more to him later as the Ravager War intensified, but there was always a part of him that assumed the plan would go wrong because so often initial plans did.

It was usually the next phases that paid off. He'd counted on it.

That knowledge was integral to being a successful businessman and helped him to remain wise in general. And if things didn't go wrong, then he would enjoy a drink even more so afterward.

Enginsan had given Colonel Horne a long leash of belief. Horne thought of the colonization of the planet as a mission and under the umbrella of the military.

For soldiers, accomplishing the mission was the priority, mission first and all of that, and how it happened, there was usually a lot of gray area for improvisation.

It was in that gray area that Enginsan protected himself and his many businesses.

Enginsan had allowed Horne to believe that he had control over the mission and also the protection of the military, but to Enginsan, the planet was just his next business venture, another planet to add to his collection.

He owned one and desperately wanted another. He'd yet to decide on a third.

The military was the perfect scapegoat because any lawsuits, investigations, or him being sued—for his wealth, wealth that ironically came mostly from weapons development—would point back to the people who were wearing uniforms.

Because of what happened, there were many deaths, but he made sure everyone had signed a copious amount of documents expressing their willingness to sacrifice themselves—and also family members, if it came to that—for the opportunity to explore and potentially colonize a new planet.

If the paperwork couldn't sustain his invisibility, then it could all be protected by ten letters—as many initials that made up the name of the operation that they signed up for, which was Tuhrelevim—and that was the term: classified.

Because of everything he'd planned, he was ready to dip into his savings, literally and figuratively. He couldn't help himself. He was practically giddy.

He knew he was getting ahead of himself a bit by naming the planet after himself, but it just felt like Planet Adelpa was his already.

And that those beasts had already been exterminated, regardless of whether the new initial barrages of ordnance failed.

What wouldn't fail were uncountable missiles and where they would hit; he had no plan to live anyway. There were even investors willing to buy the land at a safe distance from those potential targets.

Planet Adelpa would see the colonization he'd first envisioned, but occupied only by those who he approved of.

That was one of many aspects he'd left out when he'd approached Colonel Horne, but also most of the others. If they'd lived, and before they could claim land on the planet, they would have disappeared mysteriously.

As mysteriously as Enginsan's own wife—who finally encountered the very animals she spoke so highly of.

He looked up to view all of the Adelpa 3 fighter jets ready for takeoff for more bombardments.

The Ravagers, nor the Maulers that obeyed their commands, neither species of beast stood a chance against him.

He retired to his private room overlooking the surface of the planet and ordered a coffee, as Mero enjoyed doing, feeling like a god, eyeing a picture on the table of a shadowy form.

It was of a Ravager. The picture had been taken years ago by Nimbus. Enginsan relished the fantasy that the picture might one day be regarded as a picture taken of an extinct animal.

Before he'd introduced the next evolution.

CHAPTER 8

Though smaller than even an adolescent Ravager by being a Mauler, it was also smaller than most Maulers because of its older age.

Even its head wasn't the same as most of its kind because it was missing an ear. It had been bitten off during the conflict with its predecessor.

It wasn't just the ear it had lost; it had almost lost its life, but that hadn't reduced its influence over those it commanded because it survived. What it went through actually made it more powerful.

Powerful enough to survive the multiple invasions by the humans, and even live through their human weapons, the name of one of them being devil.

The devils were fired at it by a human riding on one of the vehicles during a great battle. One of the uncountable projectiles nearly obliterated a front fang.

But it had survived the battle, survived the humans, survived their destructive weapons, and the lower part of its damaged fang remained.

From then on, it proudly thought of itself as Deviltooth.

For those alive, and especially those that had been commanded, and those who'd yet to be commanded, they understood Deviltooth to be their commander, and in every way, a command by it was a command by Ravager General.

As it trotted forward, risking colliding with much younger versions of its kind but also Ravagers, its presence was sighted. The disruption it caused was purposeful.

The effect was the much larger and stronger pawing all four

paws backward to get out of its way, out of respect.

Sure, clawed groupings that had been in place since summoning their arrival—by barks, first by it, then from its underlings—dispersed from whichever direction it chose, and doing so immediately.

It meant to cause the disruption, a reminder of who was in charge.

But still under the rule of Ravager General, it must remember.

For now.

Even Deviltooth didn't always think of Ravager General still ruling, because so much had changed in its mind because of its plans, but for the time being, it still must abide by what was in place.

Many of them had never seen Deviltooth. That was also purposeful. They'd only heard of it and heard it barking commands. There was a plan and it wanted to present itself at the most optimal time.

That time turned out to be now because once again, there was a threat from the humans and it was time for Deviltooth to lead them into battle.

Before Deviltooth was commander, Ravager General had chosen its second in command, and had been its predecessor.

Before Deviltooth killed that predecessor, it had respected it, but not enough to remain under its command.

Its predecessor was not the strongest Mauler nor was it the wisest. And Ravager General had showed wisdom when it had accepted Deviltooth as its predecessor's replacement.

Deviltooth was one of the oldest Maulers that still fought. Battle scarred, battle hardened, and also wise about battle.

Maulers and Ravagers fighting together, staying in separate territories, had been different generationally, but recently, they'd joined together against the humans.

Relations between Maulers and Ravagers would likely change in the coming generations, but it hoped to live long enough to not only rule but also display its wisdom about battle to the young.

Once immersed among them, from then on until the battle was over, and after however many battles there were, until all battles were over, it would remain among the ranks, worming its way at the center of it all, Ravager and Mauler actions alike.

And always to give its commands under Ravager General's leadership, until it decided to act, to change things, how they were and would be, forever.

Respected among both kinds, it was especially proud that it was respected by the Ravagers even though it was a Mauler.

Because Deviltooth had chosen to show itself to the majority of underlings for the first time—so many had been born since the last battle with humans—understanding that its role and reputation and actions in battle had been barked about, it executed the prance.

CHAPTER 9

During the ten years since Nev had set booted feet on the planet, he'd gained about ten pounds. Unacceptable to military standards and even his own, indulging in too much good food and drink, but understandable. He wasn't active military anymore, he was retired.

He didn't go on as many runs as he used to, and although he hated to admit it, and wouldn't, not to fellow ex-soldiers, to his wife Kate, or even to himself in his own head, but some days it felt like everything hurt.

He was sure age had something to do with it, but it was more because of the mileage; so often he awoke feeling like he'd gotten into a fistfight the night before. One like he had with Makada. Or Nimbus. And most recently Ryke and his accomplice on the A-brid.

What was it about being on those aircraft that baited him into a fistfight anyway? Probably because of its wicked inception, and the man responsible for their mass production: Enginsan Adelpa.

Dealing with Enginsan—surely he was behind everything—was on Nev's agenda. If it were possible.

Although almost never ideal, Nev was trained to accomplish missions solo. First and foremost, he required another weapon. Any gun would do in order to sneak or even fight his way into the nearest base of operations.

Once he did that, he would take a pilot hostage and put the planet behind him for good. With nothing presently hunting him, Nev continued to twist the throttle, going as fast as the hover skiff would go.

Even if he didn't have experience driving the skiffs, everything was so automated these days, practically anyone could drive one. Many other military vehicles were also easy to operate.

He'd paid attention over the years. Following military tech would be a hobby of his for the rest of his life.

He checked his six, spying smoke, the only visible remnant of the A-brid crash from his current location.

Then he checked the outskirts around him, deciding the direction he would go would continue to be the opposite of where the A-brid had been flying, which was surely away from a base.

The high grass still grew everywhere. It flourished on the planet. The grass forest was so high in some places that it looked like blades of grass grew as high as twenty feet tall.

It was at the high grass where he'd first encountered Ravagers, so he kept his attention there, looking for any signs of teeth and claws, and steering away from wherever the grass grew highest.

It wasn't just predators Nev needed to remain wary of. Reinforcements could have been sent after the crash or even a rescue mission.

Nev doubted it, and not just because Ryke and Kilroy were assholes, but it seemed everything happening would be kept in the dark and only dragged into the light when it could be manipulated and molded according to its architects.

His survival depended on depending on contingencies.

He also knew to steer clear of any water, away from all of the dark shapes that hunted under the surface, deciding that—for his own safety—every living thing on the planet was carnivorous and hungry for humans.

It was a safe bet.

As he drove, he kept thinking about how the hell he'd gotten himself into such a mess, even with all of the precautions he'd taken.

The mystery of waking up on the A-brid with no recollection of his abduction and transportation was similar to the same plan to frame him before, before he'd realized that the military operation, that Operation Tuhrelevim, was just a smokescreen.

Why would he be left for dead again? How much had it cost

Enginsan and whoever else to transport him here? Why not just shoot him on sight, many miles away, and away from the planet?

Nev remembered what had happened, the devastation on the planet, why didn't they? Enginsan and his wealthy cronies must simply be blinded by their grudge against him.

After surviving the fistfight with Nimbus, Nev had made his way back to Fort Beckett, and that was when he'd first observed the Maulers, so based on past experience, it was very important that he be ready for anything.

He'd survived the planet before, whatever it was currently called or would be named in the future, so he would do the same as he did back then, because he must.

And it definitely helped that a military mind frame was a gear that he could always shift down to, retired or not.

Having a strong memory was part of that gear, so he'd memorized the map of the territory, and also he had much more experience driving a skiff since first arriving on the planet over ten years ago.

Every skiff was equipped with a tool box and within them were binoculars. Once he could do so safely, he would withdraw them to get a better look at his surroundings.

CHAPTER 10

The prance was exhausting to display to so many but it was a necessary show of strength, a proud coordination of movement that impressed, always with a front paw and a back paw up in the air.

Not all of them could, or would even attempt it, because of what it signified.

It had been something Deviltooth needed to practice alone to get right. It was not so young anymore.

Maulers lowered their heads, some reluctantly, following along with what the others were doing, but even Ravagers did as well.

Deviltooth executed the prance because it understood what its Mauler predecessor had not; the prance of Ravager General was something only Ravager leaders did and was respected among Ravagers.

Because of their subservience over the generations, Maulers simply fell in line with them.

And showing something familiar that Ravager Generals did was a guise of subservience on its part. That was also part of its plan.

The display of power was also servility. It also showed compliance, compromise, strength and decency, and that they were all on the same side even though Maulers and Ravagers were different.

Prancing showed them that it understood everything the display signified, but Deviltooth believed something it would never bark about. The prance was weak, a weakness that it would end, and was a necessary step toward it ruling.

That direction was forward into the future, past the point of failure and losing battles. What it envisioned doing was making motions similar to the humans wearing their uniforms and saluting one another; a new custom.

The custom of the prance was one that Deviltooth would eliminate whenever it was possible.

Something else it thought but didn't bark; the prance was a ruse it would use to one day divide them.

It couldn't let on how much it had to concentrate on every move of the prance as it continued.

Although Deviltooth was old, every flaw would be forgiven by those witnessing it because it remained spry and never hesitated to exact attacks itself, for strategy, or for revenge.

It concentrated on what it knew itself to be; hardened, tough, uncompromising, and unequivocally ferocious.

Every moment it was leading, it understood that it was best to side with the Ravagers rather than being at war with them.

But only until the humans were wiped out.

It led by example to show the young—all became aware of the differences between Ravagers and Maulers early—and showed them the best way would be its way.

Another way to lead and show its power and continue to be in power was always to be at the forefront of the battling.

That was something it never shied away from. It was always ready for conflict. Always.

It wasn't just consistent positioning by strategy, contemplating new strategies, and implementing strategies that maintained its position and respect by the others, it was Deviltooth being watched during the fighting and remembered.

It had fought so much that it earned the respect of its fellow Maulers, and the Ravagers as well. Attaining its role as commander was also proven by way of its appearance. The result of its ascent through the ranks were many scars.

Although none of them could understand a certain strategy but itself, the previous Mauler commander had taken off one of its ears while Deviltooth implemented that particular one—before Deviltooth had killed it—the goal was a planned new future.

Advancing when it wasn't ready, using its teeth and claws more ferociously than it had ever done during its life, and ripping the throat out of Mauler Commander, their leader, its leader, had been a betrayal of the worst kind.

The wounds from doing so were still felt by it, mentally and physically.

It couldn't communicate that temporary subservience would allow absolute power. Few could understand something like it were even possible, and fewer would believe it was possible at all.

Throughout its life and even to itself sometimes, it sometimes doubted its own strategies. Before believing in them again. The events and aftermath told truths.

It taking the role of commander, leader of the Maulers, had severed the constant war between Maulers and Ravagers. That war had gone on for so many generations that not even it was aware of how many.

Long before it was born.

Now because of what it had done, seemingly yielding, viewed as a betrayer to its own kind, the Maulers followed the Ravagers, and that was its goal.

What Deviltooth wanted for its kind was what all Maulers did, to live on, and under previous leadership—the whims of Ravagers, especially Ravager General—the Maulers would eventually be slaughtered to the last of their kind.

Its next strategy would be executed soon. Ravager General was more vulnerable now that it was missing an eye. If Ravager General remained in power, humans would one day rule this world, and that was something it would not allow.

The prance was but one attempt to eat away at Ravager General's power, and Deviltooth would also need to compete its hardest until that very power belonged to it alone.

It craved to be able to do what it saw Ravager General do once; stomp a massive clawed paw and every Mauler and Ravager within view of it lowered their heads with respect.

After doing what needed to be done, Deviltooth would only need give a look for the same reaction.

CHAPTER 11

"Are we the only mercs to have seen more than reported?" Three-one asked.

Two-one gave him a look. "Don't call us that."

"Call us what?"

"Mercs."

"*They* call us that."

"Who's *they*?"

"Everyone in orbit. It's what we are. Huh? Just answer the question."

"Which one? I'm confused."

"Shocker. Are *we* the only ones to have seen the most?"

"I think so. Without *evidence*."

"Well, we *did* see them. That's the evidence."

"Yeah, but they don't see it that way."

"What would entail so called evidence?"

"Live capture."

"That ain't happening at our level."

"Or a dead body to haul in or a thousand we could take a picture of. Something we can prove."

"Just glimpses of reported movement isn't enough to get higher off their asses?"

"Apparently not, but then again, everything seems to move around here."

"And getting remotely close for further proof isn't worth the risk. They're faster than they look."

"Ravagers or Maulers?"

"Both."

"You said it."

"What if we sent pictures of dead Burrowers?"

"They don't care about them. They already said so."

"If it were Mero sending the intel, they'd jump through their asses if he told them to. And jump as far as he told them to."

"Huh? Never mind."

"What did higher say during the last transmission? What was the update? I was relieving myself."

"Yeah, I know. I was watching your six."

"How did they respond?"

"I only got as far as the R-T-O. I don't even know if he was ex-military like us. Some civilian. All polite and stuff."

"What did the civvy say?"

"That we're being paranoid and to focus on the mission."

"He told you that?"

"Someone told him to tell him that."

"Did you tell him that missions are for soldiers and our goal is to get paid as much as possible?"

"I should have."

"How can you be polite and say we're being paranoid and to focus? That doesn't sound polite to me. It sounds rude."

"It was how calm he was. His tone."

"Oh. But isn't what we're doing here focusing on the mission?"

"I know. It's stupid. He was stupid. *Is* stupid."

"I'm gonna kick his ass. What did you say his name was?"

"I didn't. He didn't." Two-one's brow furrowed. "And since when is everyone on a first name basis over the radio?"

Three-one shrugged. "Just want to kick some ass is all. Do *something* fun while we're here."

"At least we're getting paid a ton for what is essentially guard duty."

"I haven't been on guard duty since I was active duty. The funny part is them ignoring *our* instincts."

"Because they don't know us."

"We're being hunted."

"No kidding."

"As a whole, I mean. We humans."

"At least, we'll witness the attack from afar, not be the first to get torn up."

"I'd rather not get torn up at all."

"You know what I meant. Report to higher they're about to get their asses chewed, literally."

"Yeah, chewed off." Three-one laughed. "We should just contact Mero. He'll come here and do what's necessary. What needs to be done. What we want them to do. They'll believe *him*."

"Yeah, but then he'll be here with us. He tends to stick around. Do we really want that?"

"Not really. I don't know why he likes to practice hunting everything. Even us. Gives me the creeps."

"He practices on practically everything that moves."

"That's what I just said."

"The guy's a shark. If he stops, he'll die. A born hunter."

"I can't stand mercs like him. Now that guy's a merc; I don't care what you say."

"Careful."

"There's too much flat terrain. He isn't nearby. Even if he is, he'd only be able to see us, not hear us."

"If you say so."

"Whatever. Stop messing with me. I hate how he likes to break people down too, when he's with you, psychoanalyzing and all that."

"He's type A."

"So are we."

"Are we?"

"I've been told I was."

"They probably meant *asshole* but didn't finish their sentence."

"Fuck off. I've met plenty of people like him who don't do what he does."

"What do you mean?"

"Put people off. Piss them off. Make them hate him. Stupid of him. I'm tired of his bullshit. Thinks he can chew out anybody for any reason. I don't wear a uniform anymore."

"Well, kind of."

"I mean no rank. No enlistment papers. And I'll never salute anybody again. Especially that asshole. Somebody might need to save his ass one day. That somebody might be one of us."

"I doubt it. For some reason, he strikes me as the type who'll never need saving."

"Well, no one lives forever. Tough, well-trained, *and* rich. I hate that guy. Why's he even here?"

"Why do you think? His currency, man. Those accounts are deep and decades old. And he wasn't the founder. Daddy's money."

"Granddaddy."

"Whatever. Once the construction begins on what they promised him, he can just show up."

"Begins again."

"What?"

"Once construction begins *again*. They've tried this before, remember?"

"I wasn't here, remember? And it wasn't like they started on Mero's palace way back when."

"They're going to build him a palace?"

"Something like that. Maybe it was a resort."

"A resort. Like he's going to have guests?"

"I don't know."

"There's no way he has friends, so it's gotta be some situation where he's taking advantage of people."

"Hunt them down probably."

Three-one laughed. "How do you know all this?"

"Oh, I've heard things."

"Tell me."

"Nah, it doesn't matter. It'll just piss you off compared to what we get."

"Besides his money, Mero just wants to prove himself. That's all there is to it."

"Prove himself to who?"

"Himself. And to relatives who are long dead, who he looks up to, who he's never met. I wish my grandfather paved the way for *my* legacy."

"And we're stuck with him."

"Don't worry, we won't be on this planet forever."

"Yeah, we can just stay if we want to, but if we don't get this done, who would want to?"

CHAPTER 12

Two-one and Three-one eyed the empty landscape with jagged mountains that looked like teeth in the distance everywhere they looked.

They were armed with standard Rovla assault rifles. No scopes. No rails decked out with nonsense. Just iron sights and extra magazines stuffed into ammo pouches decorating the light gear they wore.

That gear was light and fit to fight. No armored plates inserted into the front and back of their LBVs, no helmets being worn, just practical weapon of choice and plenty of ammo.

The enemy wasn't human, so bullets weren't a threat, nor were explosives, just teeth and claws, and also wicked intelligence according to all those redundant briefings.

"There's another one," Three-one said. "See it?"

Two-one looked. The movement was quick but it was the unmistakable form of a quadruped predator squeezing itself out of the ground, a brief gallop, tail flipping, and then it disappeared over a rise.

"A Mauler. I saw it. Great. Ready?"

"I suppose."

There was hesitation on his battle buddy's part, so Two-one glanced in the distance, and there was the slightest hint of life. He almost missed it. There was a beast on a hill and facing them. Ravager or Mauler he couldn't tell.

When Two-one raised small binoculars, the magnification showed it was gone. "Man, this ain't good."

"What?"

"Nothing," Two-one said. "Come on."

Two-one and Three-one raised Rovla rifles and range-walked forward, eyeing the slope of the rise where the Mauler had disappeared.

"Jeez, what are the chances it's going to turn back and see—"

"*Shh*. Look."

They halted. Another animal corpse, just like many they'd seen, and killed by a horrible mauling. But the Mauler that was surely responsible wasn't in sight. Just the hole in the ground it had crawled out of.

"See it anywhere?"

"Negative."

"Where the hell did it go?"

"No idea."

"Another dead Burrower."

Both mercs eyed it. Burrowers were about the size of a Mauler but an herbivore. They had flat teeth, small useless eyes, and long claws for digging.

"Holy hell. Do you know what this means?"

"Tell me."

"That must be how they seemed to appear out of nowhere."

"They meaning them?"

"Yeah. What did higher say at first a decade ago? That they thought they were traveling across the mountains to mask their body heat."

"A dumb theory."

"No kidding. They've dug deep underground caverns to travel undetected."

"Or it was dug already."

"Regardless, they can move underground. And they obviously understand that we don't want to harm the planet because we want to live here. Humans, I mean."

"Whoa, guilty conscience. Don't involve me in your plot."

"It means they know why we're here but also our limits."

"I'm here just to get paid. Not psychoanalyze critters. And also no way. They're just animals."

"Try another report."

"Waste of time. Seriously all that matters is that we're getting paid, right?"

"Tell that to Mero."

His fellow merc replied with a *pfft*. He keyed his shoulder mic. "Base, this is Perimeter Two-one."

"Go ahead, Two-one."

"We found another dead animal."

"Is that him?" Three-one said, stepping on the RTO's response. "The guy I'm going to beat up?"

Two-one reared back with a fake punch. "Shut up, I can't hear." He keyed the mic. "Say again?"

Three-one grinned and allowed his Rovla to dangle from the strap in front of him, raised clenched fists again, and punched at the air, pretending what he'd like to do to the RTO.

"I say again: what kind of animal?"

Two-one shook his head. "Burrower."

Net static was his response.

"Base, was my report understood?"

Swirling static.

"Fucking comms. Forget it."

"Look."

Two-one looked where Three-one pointed, done goofing off. There was a crack in the planet, a jagged rocky mouth yawning at the horizon, a cave that seemed to have been dug even bigger judging by the piles of dirt and rocks at the front of it.

"Looks like something big came out of there."

"Or wanted in, in a hurry."

"Probably many somethings."

"Watch my six." Two-one grabbed a grenade off of his LBV and hustled back the way they'd come.

"Where are you going?" Three-one called after him. "What are you doing?"

Two-one pulled the pin and tossed the grenade down the hole where the Mauler had appeared from before.

Seconds later there was an explosion underground, shaking the ground beneath their feet, but obscuring the hole.

"It isn't blocked completely."

"But if something tries to get out, we'll see."

"OK. But doing things like that are probably going to piss them off."

"They aren't pissed off already?"

"Even more pissed off."

"What choice do we have, get attacked with our backs turned while we're messing with radios that should have solid comms but don't? Don't you think comms should work out here at this point?"

"What do you think I think?

"Before *we* went here again. Before *they* got this far again. Shouldn't they have worked this part out? It's just basic shit. Don't do dumb shit. How hard is that? All of it should be a go before the heavy lifting. That way they don't get us all killed. And themselves killed. Like the last time."

"Speaking of not doing dumb shit, how about try base again?"

"You have a radio."

"They listen to you."

"Might as well. Base, this is Perimeter Two-one." He waited for a response. "It'll fix itself. Why don't we go over to that cave."

"Famous last words."

"It's closer to base. I'll bet comms is better."

"If I were smart, I'd take that bet."

"Good thing you're as dumb as the rest of us." Two-one peered around briefly. "Let's keep our radios on, so we can keep our trigger fingers where they belong."

"You sure?"

"Yeah."

"At least I'll have someone to blame if we say the wrong thing and they hear it."

"That sounds like you."

"Up yours."

"All right, I'm done venting."

"What a relief."

"Whatever. Follow my lead."

CHAPTER 13

Three-one waved his hand in front of his face after only a few steps. "Smell that?"

Two-one didn't react. "What do you think."

The scent of death was practically a visible fog and lingered at the edge of the cave. Just inside the cave, and likely far deeper, there were dead Burrowers. There were so many. It had been a slaughter. There was a trail of them leading in.

"This isn't hunting, this is just killing."

"They wanted them dead. Wanted them out of their way."

"What's that sound? Oh man."

There were Burrower pups squealing pathetically near one that had probably been their mother, and they were likely starving to death.

Two-one looked to Three-one. "We should—"

"Yeah."

"I just can't do them little ones."

"I'll do it quick."

"Thanks, man."

Three-one did his best to mask his disgust after removing his side arm. He put a bullet in every one of their heads, putting them out of their misery.

"How many of them do you think there are?"

Three-one holstered his sidearm. "Just what we see here, thousands, but who knows."

"There were probably a lot more but they likely fled after Maulers started killing them."

"Not Ravagers?"

"Either or."

"Fled where? I didn't see any on the run."

Two-one shrugged. "Burrowers use their claws to dig underground, creating massive caves that run in all directions under Adelpa's surface, right? They probably went deeper."

"Does that make sense?"

"Not really."

"Should we head inside?"

"What the hell else are we going to do? We're getting paid no matter what, right?"

"As long as we survive."

"Thanks for that."

"We should know more about what to do next when comms is back up. Maybe we should wait for that to happen. It's just—"

"What?"

"I get the feeling we're not alone. But I don't see anything out here, which means the obvious. They're in there."

"What would they be doing in there? Why wait? There's just two of us."

Three-one didn't have an answer.

"I'd rather have eyes on what's hunting us, so I know where to aim."

"I agree."

"Earn those bonuses."

"Maybe Mero will let us stay at his resort."

"I doubt it."

"Then we'll throw eggs at it and then run away and laugh like idiots. Now I'm hungry."

"Me too. We'll have MREs once we're back in the sunshine."

"If we survive."

Two-one laughed nervously. "Let's move."

Both flicked on the flashlights attached to their LBVs, slowly growing more light into the darkness with every step, splashing it in multiple directions.

Due to the slope, the cave ceiling looked a hundred feet high, and the bodies of the Burrowers were practically piled, and those piles were everywhere. Thankfully, there were no more live pups to deal with.

“All of them grimacing. You notice that?”

“Yeah.”

“What do you think it means?”

“Are you kidding?” Two-one yell whispered. “They tried to fight off what killed them.”

“This cave could be hundreds of miles long.”

“Or longer.”

“How far should we go?”

“Until we encounter a situation we can’t get ourselves out of. Or something worthy of intel to report to higher other than dead animals.”

“Yeah, something that might get them off their asses.”

“I wouldn’t mind hearing some Adelpa 3s heading our way.”

“You said it. Do you think they just heard our request?”

Tilting his head toward the radio mic on his shoulder, there was still static. “I doubt it.”

“This is all wrong.”

“What is?”

“Burrowers know where to dig so as not to not disturb the surface or give away their location. But that doesn’t matter to a Mauler. Or likely a Ravager.”

“It’s not like Ravagers and Maulers are enemies. They’re on the same team.”

“Yeah, but this is sloppy. Like they were in a hurry.”

“Maybe avoiding ordnance?”

“Yeah, but that hasn’t happened for a while and not at this location.”

“Maybe it’s only this way because this is the only entrance. The Ravagers must know they’re going to be attacked somehow.”

“Do you think it was the ordnance dropped on them in their territory that was their first clue?”

“Smartass. I meant before that. They killed Burrowers and took their home for their own survival. Somehow they know what we’re going to do.”

“From what I’ve heard, they’re smart enough to figure it out as long as they see us here. They talk."

"Talk?"

"Bark or whatever."

"I haven't seen a Ravager. Just those Maulers."

"But they're in charge."

"They?"

"The Ravagers."

"We need to report what we've discovered to higher."

"We haven't discovered anything. And we're broadcasting."

"You know what I mean. What we've figured out. Should we keep going? If we do, we most definitely won't get any comms. Not in here."

"We've seen enough. Let's hump it out to where there definitely will be comms. And if there still isn't, we'll just keep heading for base."

"I get the feeling we'll only get comms when we're standing inside the wire."

A growl caused both mercs to snap their Rovla rifles into aiming positions, but there was only darkness to aim at.

Another rumbly growl, this time sounding like it was coming from another location, beside them.

Then another, from behind them.

"We're being hunted."

"You think so?" Three-one whispered. "Let's get the fuck out of here."

They slowly backed out of the intricately dug tunnels, as if the Maulers and Ravagers had been born to exterminate the Burrowers, take over their homes, and live underground, and it had always been their territory.

"They planned this. They must have been hiding under the dead. In case we—"

Two-one's face disappeared inside a clawed paw and he yelled in a way that no grown man should have.

Three-one rushed forward, aiming his Rovla at the Ravager's back, wanting to save his fellow merc, his friend.

But he never fired a shot because he found himself slammed

onto his back after his legs were clawed out from under him. Another Ravager pushed its mouth against his stomach, chewing and biting.

It must have hit an artery because when it yanked its head out, it was drenched in his blood.

The Ravager shook its head back and forth, tossing droplets everywhere, raining the cave with steaming red.

CHAPTER 14

Ravagers and Maulers were underground. To kill them beneath the surface would damage the planet itself, and the animals knew it. Humans build up. Apparently, animals on other planets besides Earth can build down too.

Thankfully Nev's radio had been on the right frequency. The mercs made their radios open frequency, an attempt to combat shitty comms so higher would hear it and contact them.

They must not have considered other radios nearby could pick up their chatter. Unfortunately Nev had to listen to what happened to one or both of them. Torn apart by a beast was probably one of the worst ways to die. Nev had seen it happen firsthand.

His first instinct had been to locate the vehicle the mercs had been driving, their frequency acting as a beacon for him to hone in on, but after what happened to them, he decided against heading their way and avoid the same fate.

He also considered contacting the base the mercs failed, to communicate their findings, to relay what they'd discovered and seen, also what had happened to them, anonymously, if possible.

But whoever they were trying to communicate with weren't exactly keen on being much help, and their vehicle was located close to where they'd been killed, and Nev knew what had killed them. He wasn't going there. And that was his old way of thinking.

There were people on this planet who'd been involved in plotting his abduction, and if Nev and Kate hadn't been so diligently prepared, then she would be there with him or dead.

Because Kate was considered a loose end in such a conspiracy, that they'd involved her, Nev didn't owe anybody on this planet anything. Every human was on his or her own and that included himself.

Kate had been through enough. Both of them went through therapy after what happened.

Kate had become quite the kickboxer since, even bloodying Nev's lip when he prodded her to show him what she could do. To her shock and then her laughter.

He could think on happy memories later.

Nev remembered thinking that the Ravagers had been underground when there were so many, when there were millions advancing on Fort Beckett and when the Adelpa 3 fighter jet crashed.

The sound of their victorious roaring.

Because there had to be an additional way that they had appeared, not just across the landscape, underground was likely how many of the beasts moved toward Fort Beckett during Operation Tuhrelevim.

They'd done then what they were doing now, displacing Burrowers from their underground homes in order to survive. No doubt Burrowers had fought back but were killed back then too.

It was impossible for the underground dwellers to survive attacks by Ravagers or Maulers, and it also meant that the beasts could be underfoot at all times. Nev would remain battle ready.

He reflected how different things were. When he was stationed at Fort Beckett specifically, the military base had been fully operational, the planet a deployment destination for soldiers—since space travel was figured out a long time ago.

All of the familiar camaraderie known to a former soldier like Nev had ended. Being stationed on the planet in the traditional sense was in the past. Almost as if it had never happened.

Nev wondered what the status of Fort Beckett was but rationalized it was abandoned and likely destroyed. He remembered the final battle well and Colonel Mathis fighting heroically to allow Nev and Kate to board the Adelpa 4.

Even though Fort Beckett had been geared up to run on its own for years, no doubt it was in shambles. He'd likely only find dilapidated and abandoned military weapons and equipment, including Adelpa launchers.

Whatever was left had probably been taken over by vegetation and completely obscured by now.

It wasn't worth the drive to see if he could find any weapons or equipment of use. He would likely have access to everything he needed soon from somewhere else.

Colonel Mathis had been like Nev, in that he was innocent in all that had happened, the conspiracy, and Nev was grateful for Mathis's sacrifice. If it weren't for him, Nev and Kate might not be alive.

Sergeant Major Kayner had probably been innocent in the corruption during the mission as well, and also—even though he was an asshole—Major Makada. It was just those at the tip of the spear who were corrupt.

And Enginsan was most definitely the pointy tip of all that greed.

Locating the base the mercs referred to was hardly difficult after parking the skiff a distance away and getting eyes on it with binoculars located in the toolbox attached. The base didn't have a name that he could see, not like the sign at Fort Beckett.

Not that he expected a sign; the personnel weren't active military, but definitely were prior service, like Ryke and Kilroy and the pilot on the A-brid had been. It was obvious by the way they walked.

There weren't many who were walking though, many of them drove Adelpa rovers, all-terrain vehicles used for military operations, but were also sold to civilians for their pleasure.

They were reminiscent of the four-wheeled all-terrain vehicles from Earth during previous wars, and some of the vehicles didn't have a roof, just like the one he'd confiscated from another pair of mercs miles from the base after abandoning the skiff.

Luckily for Nev, there were multiple battle buddy teams on patrol. Not wanting to kill them, he had knocked both of them out and grabbed one of their Rovla assault rifles. They'd wake up soon, but Nev planned to be off planet by then.

He'd swiped a merc's helmet, too, and wore it to obscure his face. The uniform would help him blend in with the rest of the mercenaries.

Not only was the merc he'd stolen it from going to wake up with a serious headache, he'd also be quite chilly since Nev stripped him down to his underwear. No doubt his battle buddy would give him shit when he came to.

Even though many of the personnel were ex-military, it was jarring to experience the world without an obvious military bearing. There was a casualness to conversation, appearance, and overall a relaxed demeanor.

It was strange to remember all of the seemingly beneficial missions he and his fellow soldiers had gone on while stationed there. Now the only humans occupying the planet, ex-military or not, were essentially civilians.

Remembering those missions made Nev angry. Because of so many coverups, especially the main mission, which was to locate missing soldiers that higher was very aware of and what happened to them after they'd gone missing.

They'd been killed by the beasts.

Nev hated the residual feelings of failure even though what happened and everything that had gone wrong wasn't his fault and was a long time ago. He'd simply wanted to complete the mission, protect his soldiers, and protect his wife.

And also survive. He'd liked his life.

From where he was positioned, there were no launchers that he could see, just aircraft. Any catastrophic weapons intended for what was going on were likely arriving from orbit.

But it also meant that everything going on was intended to be mobile, even though there was a runway. It looked like some lessons from facing the dominant life forms on this planet hadn't been forgotten.

There were likely transport ships loaded with building materials, people, those who considered themselves elite, but they were no doubt on standby. Nothing substantial would land again until it was considered safe.

People who were wide-eyed and enthusiastic about what they imagined the potential for the planet would be for them. If they only knew the truth. Nev wondered what lines of nonsense had been fed to them so that they would invest.

Driving toward the front gate, he hoped entry wouldn't be a problem. He doubted it would be. He was completely disguised. He looked like all the other men and women driving around as if the threat of teeth and claws were no longer a threat.

But they couldn't be more wrong about that. The shit was about to hit the fan. He could sense it.

Nev was even ready to pretend to act like an asshole, like Ryke, or even someone else and speak with an accent—he'd served with enough fellow soldiers to impersonate their voices—but the gate opened automatically.

Was I recognized?

A mission going smoothly, everything being too easy, was always hoped for, but when it actually happened, the part of him that would always be a soldier didn't trust it.

His current plan might have to be aborted until he thought of another one. If he had to, if there were any signs of trouble, he'd put it in reverse and speed out of there, abandon the rover, and reacquire the skiff.

Helmeted, he blended in with the rest of the arrogant humans driving around base, driving around beyond the wire, and probably anywhere else on the planet that they wanted.

Strange, the freedom of transportation was possible. He'd seen the creatures again, surely they had too. It wasn't as if beasts no longer roamed Planet Adelpa.

All at once, Nev understood how human arrogance was so possible. He hadn't even needed to look up to correctly identify the aircraft capable of low-altitude search and destroy missions.

He heard the unmistakable sound of an Adelpa 3 fighter jet slicing through the sky, leaving a powerful echo in its wake.

Nev spotted another Adelpa 3 in the distance. Airspace patrols were definitely a solid way to keep beasts at bay.

Remaining still behind the wheel as he slowly drove inside, he saw a golden light scanning the windshield coming from the side of the open gate, scanning a barcode he hadn't noticed before.

Enginsan obviously hired people only loyal to him, so of course Nev wasn't given a worthy inspection. Really those men and women were loyal only to Enginsan's wealth, and security was lacking.

Nev straightened the smirk forming on his lips upon the realization that a former captain, the man responsible for ending Operation Tuhrelevim, actually drove into the enemy base.

CHAPTER 15

The gate closed behind him, which meant three things.

One, there were only people driven by greed and other petty motivations stationed on the planet because there was practically zero operational security. What he'd just done, proved it.

Two, the rest of the life on Planet Adelpa were mostly comprised of highly intelligent beasts who wanted to eliminate the people on the planet.

And three, all of that made it really easy for Nev to do whatever was necessary against anyone who got in his way.

All of his next decisions would be easy ones. The question was how difficult it would be to accomplish them.

Going into the nearest warehouse sized building as if he belonged there, Nev was irritated to find that it was not a warehouse storing what he hoped for, which was a variety of weapons, but a lab.

Nev was surprised to see there was only one person. He glanced around, expecting more. The man was some kind of doctor by the way he was dressed. He didn't seem like a soldier.

Except he wasn't exactly alone. He was walking toward a cage with a Ravager inside of it.

"What the hell is going on here?" Nev couldn't help blurting out the question. "Are you out of your mind?"

The doctor turned around, a prickly look on his face. "May I help you?"

Nev thought quickly. He slung the strap attached to the Rovla over his shoulder. "Sorry, I've just never seen anyone so comfortable around them."

The doctor stared. "Have you not been on this planet for very long?" A prickly expression also edged his tone. "You don't need to wear your helmet in here."

"No thanks. I don't want to get into trouble. Or take up any of your time."

"Any more of my time you meant."

"Right. It's just that I've been here long enough to wonder what the heck goes on in here. I always wondered. I just had to know. Interesting stuff."

Nev suddenly wondered if his age would give him away. He just hoped his physical condition made him seem like all the other young mercs who were in tip-top shape.

He considered telling a fake name. He was prepared to do so, but the doctor didn't have a nametag. It seemed everyone who knew he was in there would know him.

Nev should do the same, but he was relieved when the doctor turned back toward the cage.

"Then you'll find this captivating."

The doctor reached into the cage, past the bars, and actually touched the Ravager. In fact, it looked like he was petting it.

Ravagers looked even bigger indoors, huge, especially inside a cage that was too small for it. But then again, no animal meant to hunt clever prey belonged in a cage.

Nev realized that the doctor had no idea who he was, that he couldn't have known his story, and really believed he was just some merc who'd stumbled inside the lab, so Nev continued the ruse.

He stepped closer. "Fascinating."

The doctor put his hand inside the Ravager's mouth and—incredibly—the Ravager actually licked his hand. He removed what should have been bitten off and wiped it on his white lab coat. Saliva glistened.

"Now prepare to be impressed."

The doctor crouched to the floor, and using a surgical saw in hand, he used it to trim down one of the Ravager's claws until the pointy tip of it fell forward.

Standing, he threw the tip of the claw into the air, and caught it, but it fell out of his grasp. He bent over and picked it up again, shoving the claw tip into a pocket on his lab coat. "Do you know how I can do that?"

He obviously just wanted someone to talk to. Who knew how often he worked alone. Maybe all the time. Nev only just met him and he was annoyed by him. Silently, he questioned his sanity.

"No idea."

"The birth of her pup was strained."

Nev looked where he was pointing. He hadn't seen the Ravager pup also in the cage. It was so tiny, a miniaturized version of what was so fierce, Nev had never seen one so little before, and it looked like everything was growing.

Awfully large paws for a pup. The difference was that it looked completely innocent, with no hint of the ferociousness of the adults, not even in its eyes.

"I helped. She remembers. She'll never harm me but do you know what would happen if *you* tried to do what I just did?"

Nev didn't have to wonder. He could tell just by the way the female Ravager watched him. "I'd be torn apart."

"Precisely. They are highly intelligent. Most of them. Not so much the young but that goes without saying. They remember faces of humans, and each other, their own kind."

If that's true, it definitely doesn't bode well for me.

"Fascinating beasts," the doctor said.

"Yet you call them beasts."

"It's what they are. We humans could be referred to the same way. Particularly throughout history."

"I agree. Especially Enginsan Adelpa."

The doctor grinned. "Even the untrustworthy sort can serve a purpose, don't you think?"

Good. No cameras.

Nev had enough of the present charade, so he decided to do something about it. He casually walked forward, continuing to act interested, until he grabbed the doctor by the collar.

"What's the meaning of this?" The doctor grimaced. "Who's your supervisor?"

"I don't have a supervisor."

"I'll inform Mr. Adelpa himself then—"

"Go ahead." Nev removed his helmet. "I'm not one of those idiots out there, I was only pretending to be. My name is Nev, formerly Captain Nev, of Operation Tuhrelevim."

The doctor's expression soured, showing he had indeed heard of the man standing before him holding his collar in clenched hands.

Nev shoved him. "Tell me what's going on here."

The doctor nearly fell after stumbling, but remained upright. "Or what?"

Nev patted the stock of the Rovla. "Or use your imagination."

"I, by instructions from Mr. Adelpa, have collected genetic samples from the beasts. He plans to crossbreed Ravagers and Maulers with a domesticated breed of animal, something more docile."

"What kind of animal? From Earth?"

"That's classified."

"Classified, huh?"

"Mr. Adelpa has decided to keep some information to himself. An exercise in futility that will likely fail, in my opinion, I informed him, but obviously he feels differently. I'm being paid to help."

"Good for you. Go on."

"Mr. Adelpa isn't just behind the planned colonization of this planet, now named after himself, but also to procure the D-N-A of Ravagers and Maulers. Early on, he was the main investor but after the encounter with the Ravagers, he took more interest. Got more involved."

Nev was reminded of how weak-willed civilians could be. That was why Nev always wished—for everyone—that they served in the military.

Doing so strengthened character and no soldier or former soldier would be willing to give up information. Not at all or so easily.

But Nev had to remember that whatever happened after the altercation, he would be dealing with the mercs, and most—or all—of them were ex-military like himself and not to be taken as lightly as some doctor.

Nev almost commanded him to explain what kind of interest Enginsan had taken in the Ravagers, what he'd meant, but he didn't have to; the look Nev gave him spurred the doctor to continue his explanation.

"My employer intends to create an army of the creatures. That way he can complete Operation Tuhrelevim, or whatever he'd rename it. He's hired mercenaries for patrols and also plans to bombard the planet with endless airstrikes. Then he plans on sending in his genetically engineered—altered—creatures to hunt down and kill the indigenous creatures until all survivors are extinct."

Such a selfish act, one only a spoiled rich person could concoct, be obsessed about, and follow through on, or even consider. Nev hated Enginsan even more, even though he'd never met him.

Nev heard enough. He'd been in enough fights to know where to punch someone to knock them out. He reached out, grabbing the doctor by the arm, and swung at his jaw, clipping it solidly, reeling him in as he fell, and laying his head softly on the floor.

It was then Nev noticed oversized body bags in a separate room large enough to fit dead Ravagers or Maulers. Some of them rose up with something inside of them. It was a morgue.

He regretted handling the doctor so delicately.

CHAPTER 16

Nev was impressed by one of Enginsan's strengths, which was that he designed what he distributed himself. He began his career as a weapons manufacturer and inventor and eventually became a weapons dealer, which included artillery and aircraft.

Shady but skilled.

Enginsan must want plain old revenge against him. Revenge for Nev's interference in his plans. What the doctor had revealed about crossbreeding was and likely had always been Enginsan's next move.

Enginsan and the other investors weren't about to let Planet Adelpa go no matter the cost. They wanted the planet for their own purposes so badly that they were willing to wipe out all of its life in order to make that happen.

Except they obviously didn't want to damage the planet, or at least not much more than they already had. Which likely meant more mercs would be sent here in the future.

Nev hesitated about what to do next.

To his surprise, but especially that of the pup's mother's, the pup left the full grown Ravager's protection, leaving her sudden nervousness behind, squeezed through the bars, and trotted toward Nev. It must have been a secret it could do that.

Even as a pup, the Ravager had large paws and was solid with muscle but its stripes weren't showing yet. It reminded Nev of the solidness of the Mauler he'd killed after being arrested, before escaping the stockade at Fort Beckett.

The pup immediately started biting at his boots, tugging at the laces, but not aggressively, it was playful and inquisitive.

It rolled onto its back and pawed at the air with all four of them and gnashed with its teeth, practicing what it would do very effectively in the future.

Nev visibly unslung the Rovla and set it on the floor. He bent down and patted it lightly and then rubbed its belly as it squirmed under his hand.

Glancing up, Nev saw nervousness turn into worry and then into fear. It was, especially in those judgmental and intelligent eyes. She was afraid Nev was going to hurt her pup, and of course she should be. No doubt she'd seen or could smell what was in the morgue.

She was completely still and hunched low on powerful legs, paws spread out as if trying to signal to her pup for a welcome return, and also how ready she was to pounce.

Except she was locked in a cage.

And that was when Nev heard her. She wasn't growling, not exactly, more like a rumbling, a pleading warning, to both Nev—who she would maul—and her pup that it was in danger.

The pup finally grew bored of Nev and trotted toward its mother.

When Nev stood, he placed a hand on the counter and accidentally tipped over a glass of water, what the doctor must have been drinking.

It startled the pup and it ran up the nearby wall, pushed off and jumped over Nev's hand, and landed its clawed paws on the counter, emitting a baby snarl, its upper and lower lips vibrating against teeth that looked too large for its mouth.

With ferocity before calming down.

"Nice reflexes."

It blinked when he spoke. It was trembling and wide-eyed and scared standing on its four small bare, muscular legs.

"It's all right," Nev said. "I only spilled the water." Nev pointed. "See? Only water."

The pup tentatively walked over to the water, lowered, sniffed, and then licked at it, drinking.

Noticing there was water dripping, pooling below the counter onto the floor, it landed and began drinking that up as well. It was very thirsty.

Then it winced as droplets fell onto its head between its small ears, causing it to look up and dart to the side, avoiding the next drop.

Nev was amazed. It trusted him enough to drink right next to his boot. It angered him. Humans were not to be trusted.

Someone like that bastard Ryke would kill it for pleasure, and do the same to the defenseless Ravager in the cage, without even thinking twice.

Nev used some food, some meat, meant for the full grown Ravager to offer, and the pup yanked the entire piece of meat out of his hand, chomping loudly.

Sensing trust forming between him and it made him feel guilty, as if he had spoiled its existence.

The Ravager was very young though. Maybe it would forget. It hadn't even grown into its large paws. The pup squeezed back through the bars and started biting at its mother's full grown paws.

His plan began to evolve. He pulled the unconscious doctor into an empty cage and shut the door. Nev had no reason to kill him. He'd leave that up to a Mauler or Ravager that sniffed out what was going on in there.

Nev wasn't being rational, but he'd killed so many of the animals on the planet. It had been a mission, and for his own survival, but there was part of him that wanted to make amends.

And the ones that had been after him had just been defending their territory. For both sides, it wasn't personal.

Nev was no longer someone who was willing to forget himself and do the unimaginable and slaughter innocents to accomplish some mission. He had to make up for all the wrong he'd done.

The part of him that felt guilty because he was human, no matter how he rationalized his actions, propelled him over to grab the lock on the cage door.

He paused for a moment, noticing how much the face of a Ravager reminded him of an Earth lion without fur, white with dark stripes covering her, her neck rising steeply to the top of her back.

Except she weighed twice what an Earth lion did, maybe more, and she was that much more powerful. No one was meant to be this close to such a predator and live.

"I'm trusting you."

The expression on the Ravager's face did not change. He hoped he'd earned some trust by not harming her pup, and released the lock.

PART 2

Deviltooth

CHAPTER 17

Deviltooth lowered its head, feigning respect. The humans had landed. The Ravager General had allowed it without attacking. Deviltooth's confidence in their leader had changed forever.

The control Deviltooth wielded had been given to it by Ravager General after it defeated its predecessor, except it wanted all of Ravager General's power for itself.

Alone to do with it what was best, including delegating control to leaders of its choosing.

Deviltooth dispatched squads of Maulers to end the lives of half the Ravagers, that Ravager General had chosen as leaders since the last great battle against the humans. They would soon be dead.

The rest would be convinced what was best for them, which was to fall in line like the rest were about to, or else suffer the same fate.

Ravager General was the only Ravager leader with any real power now, only it didn't know it yet.

Deviltooth waited until Ravager General passed it on its blind side. The eye had been lost to the human weapons that launched into the air and exploded on the ground during one of the many battles during the past.

The same battle in which Deviltooth lost half its fang.

Oblivious to the plot underway, Deviltooth thrashed its tail and sprung, concentrating all of its strength into its powerful legs as it galloped around behind it, causing a slowdown among the ranks.

When it was close enough it leaped, both paws reaching, and clawed deep into Ravager General's remaining eye. The roar by it was pain and confusion.

All of the Ravagers went as still as water without a breeze, recognizing the challenge, waiting to side with the victor.

Now that Ravager General was completely blind, Deviltooth's Maulers went after Ravager General's rear, disorienting it more.

Dodging clawed swipes that would kill it instantly, Deviltooth launched upward and bit into the throat, hanging in the air by its bite while Ravager General and all its size and strength and ferocity raised its head into the air and tried to shake Deviltooth off.

Because its fang hadn't been destroyed completely—it was always tender and sore, often soiling its mood—it was jagged and still very sharp, perfect for gripping and ripping, but especially hanging onto flesh.

Deviltooth dangled as Ravager General's throat opened, spilling hot blood down its muzzle and body, its determined grip tested as the large Ravager thrashed and fought and growled with everything it had left, pawing with large and powerful paws that Deviltooth deflected with its own.

After so much blood loss, Ravager General wobbled, and Deviltooth opened its jaws to land on the bloody ground just in time to scramble away, just as Ravager General collapsed and rolled onto its side.

Soon afterward, Ravager General died. And Deviltooth had won.

Bloody faced, it roared victory.

Its newly won leadership would echo across the planet by barks and vocalizations by Ravagers and Maulers, and all of them would immediately understand the shift in power and what it meant: a Mauler was their leader now.

Ravager General had been their leader for far too long. In truth, and because of so many failures, they'd been leaderless.

The Ravagers—and the Maulers—had been losing to the humans since their arrival again, but everything was about to be modified.

Now both Maulers and Ravagers were Deviltooth's to command. Not that it wasn't aware there were plots without its knowledge. It would control what it could. And it would delegate.

At some point in time, another Ravager of Ravager General's size would be born, but Deviltooth would deal with it then.

CHAPTER 18

Nev ran for the exit door of the lab without bothering to look behind him, knowing that the Ravager would figure out how to get out of the cage.

How he had entered the lab became his egress and hopefully leaving would keep him alive. He couldn't go back.

And he hoped that once the Ravager escaped the warehouse, however she eventually got out, she would somehow serve as a distraction and help him escape. His plan could be executed even quicker that way. All he wanted to do was leave.

He was going with his gut and sensed mercs would aim at her over him for obvious reasons, especially because with the helmet back on he was incognito.

Still, and no matter what his intentions were, he'd keep his weapon ready to target the Ravager if he needed to. If he was wrong.

That merc, Ryke, had been right about what he'd said on the A-brid. He should have just shot Nev. He was the cause of a whole lot of trouble for them. He found himself hesitating.

Get off the planet, that was his mission.

But what if I stay for a while longer?

His decision on what to do next toggled back and forth in his mind.

Lightning quick jabs or a haymaker?

Nev was on the planet already, and even though he was retired, he wanted to stop Enginsan. He must get back to his wife, but better to do so with a clear conscience, and there were multiple paths to reach a destination.

Because he no longer was a soldier, no longer wearing a uniform displaying rank that underlings saluted, he could get some revenge too. Those experiments were wrong and stopping them landed in the right thing to do pile.

The evidence of what was being done, some sort of Ravager or Mauler hybrid, inserting them into wars in the future, was like a gut punch no matter how hard he tried to forget it.

Once a creature like that was created, there was no way they would only be used on one planet.

He thought about all of the compatriots who'd died. Even the members of Iron Sights Squad, who Nev and *his* squad had been sent to find, but hadn't even located their remains.

They'd probably been eaten or buried or both. Shortly after failing to locate them was when they'd first fought the Ravagers, at the complex.

Would Nev be betraying all his battle buddies, living or dead, by helping what they had considered to be the enemy at that time?

He didn't know. He couldn't be sure. He certainly never asked to be abducted and abandoned here again, so he had a unique opportunity.

All Nev did know, what he felt to his very core, was it was best to do what was right given current intel.

What he'd done during the past, while wearing a uniform, especially while deployed here, had been under different circumstances and had happened a long time ago. During the mission, it had been about survival according to mission parameters.

There was a big difference between doing the right thing from a certain point of view, right or wrong, as it often was when following orders, and downright abuse of power and cruelty.

Abuse of power and cruelty was what was being planned in that lab and greed was the motivator.

Enginsan thought he could benefit from the animals' aggressiveness. Harness it, use it as a weapon, for himself, and likely for sale to the highest bidder sometime in the future. Who knew what kind of weapons an evil man like him could create.

The best thing about being a soldier was that the gear tethered to a moral compass, about what was right and wrong, was accessible by result of the repetitions from being in those situations too many times to count.

Being on the right side, typically changed over time.

Current intel told Nev it needed to be tweaked since a uniform was no longer being worn, unleashing a brain that had grown since military service, that finally thought for itself, not just follow through with orders.

To do what needed to be done—he couldn't believe he was about to do this—he needed a more powerful weapon than the Rovla assault rifle he currently carried.

Puzzled, he stared at the door before him. Was it so simple? No security panel to push numbers for a security code?

He grasped the door lever, pulled down, and pushed the door itself, waiting for some sort of alarm or flashing lights or gunfire or having to punch someone he'd never met in the face, or worse, a squad of mercs ready to engage him.

There was none of that; he remained incognito, so he ducked inside, and closed the door.

"Holy shit."

Nev got chills. Not only that, he also heard himself laugh, but he quieted himself.

The place turned out to be a weapons cache. He realized he'd done this before, finding what he was looking for when he'd snuck into Fort Beckett after being left for dead the first time.

He'd been lucky back then, and even luckier this time, but luck ran out soon enough. He knew the lesson very well and would remember.

But still, he couldn't help but feel a rush; retired or not, he was a soldier through and through and always would be, and the craftsmanship of the weapons before him were works of art.

Thinking back, he had hoped that maybe he could get both hands on a weapon. In particular a specific weapon system. Because what was better than one weapon?

Two.

"Thank you, Iron Sights Squad."

It was well known that the soldiers first deployed to the planet had limited supplies and weapons. They definitely didn't have at their disposal what Nev and the rest did later for the mission.

The soldiers of Iron Sights Squad had inadvertently paved the way to more necessary—and powerful—firepower.

But just as they did, too many have died here.

Nev rebooted his bearing. The drawback to no security for entry meant someone could open the door as easily as he had, so he would need to be quick.

Except he was used to being quick, so Nev evaluated each weapon system before him, displayed as if trophies, but ones he would soon wield.

CHAPTER 19

Heads lowered with respectful fear as Deviltooth did the prance of their former leader, but by doing it this time it showed that it was their new leader, of Maulers as well as Ravagers.

Teeth and claws were curious, hesitant, because of such recent turmoil, and of course they were. It would wonder if it could take Deviltooth's place if it were them, especially considering its age.

Even Deviltooth was aware that it wasn't the most impressive of them physically, but its way would be established that the smartest led, not just the strongest.

It further sensed their inquisitiveness. It too had felt the same way when it was as young as them. Their uncertainty. Their boldness.

Because Ravager General had ruled for so long but been defeated so recently, many of them likely wondered if Deviltooth would be challenged soon.

One of the young Ravagers looked it in the eyes as it passed. A challenger.

Deviltooth, the new General, could not allow such disobedience and halted the prance. Those that would follow its commands would require the utmost discipline.

For what it had planned, that discipline must be maintained. Maulers and Ravagers alike. The alternative was failure.

Never again.

It barked in the young Ravager's direction, and a Mauler that followed Deviltooth's commands bit and tore out its throat with its teeth before the Ravager could fight back.

Deviltooth knew it could only give such a command once. The rest would be wary of the same happening to them. But it was confident it only needed to happen once.

Those in view watched it die and snarled, reporting what happened so the others out of view would know.

No others would challenge it for many days and it resumed the prance.

Deviltooth's mouth had been injured after a fang was shot during the first human invasion, but Deviltooth had still been one of the Maulers commanded by Ravager General to tear out the throats of Ravagers that failed in preventing their world from being invaded.

Now, ironically, Deviltooth was guarded by the remaining Ravagers that had replaced the Ravagers that Ravager General had deemed responsible for failing to prevent the first human invasion.

The others, Deviltooth had commanded to be killed, and was certain the last Ravager leaders were dead because the Maulers he'd barked the commands to had returned alive.

Deviltooth leered after finishing the prance, behind until he was in the middle and then finally at the front, barking orders with every clawed step, commanding them all to hunt down the humans and kill them with claws and teeth.

There would be no more waiting.

Deviltooth would engage in the forthcoming battle itself, to show by example by leading the way. It would kill more humans than any Ravagers or Maulers and show them all how it was best done.

Just as it did to the first humans that landed.

After engaging, it would withdraw to once again only give commands and lend its wisdom to the younger and inexperienced that had only brute strength and ferocity instead of experience from battle.

Ravager General had made a grave error, excluding losing its life. Because it viewed Maulers as subservient, and that Maulers served Ravagers, it had allowed Maulers to breed.

Ravager General had believed the more Maulers there were, the more that would serve Ravagers. But now Mauler numbers far outnumbered Ravagers.

After the forthcoming battle and when the humans were all dead, next to have their throats out would be all of the Ravager males.

And after them the Ravager pups, male or female.

Ravager females would serve the Maulers until their deaths.

And Maulers will reign under Deviltooth's rule.

CHAPTER 20

One of the weapon systems accessible was one he knew intimately; the M331a2, a.k.a. the Shoulder Devil. Why they were not in use meant the personnel who were proficient in handling such weaponry had not arrived.

Nev wondered how deep the ranks of mercenaries went before civilians would arrive to populate the planet. He supposed for now that didn't concern him. Because what was before him was distracting.

In view was also the close cousin to the Shoulder Devil; the M331a3.

Like many soldiers, or former soldiers, Nev was monogamous to weapon systems of choice, but he was more than willing to be unfaithful to the M331a2 for the M331a3.

Similar to the Shoulder Devil, the M331a3 had a magnetic levitation system to handle weight and recoil, and was capable of firing 20,000 rounds per minute—except from four barrels instead of a single—with a maximum load capacity of 40,000 rounds.

40,000 rounds were loaded onto the weapon itself but it could also be reloaded. How fast depended on the proximity to ammo boxes.

And similar to the Shoulder Devil, the M331a3 had a nickname; Shoulder Demon. Enginsan had brought along the big guns.

"Fucking beautiful."

By delivering the weapons, and also everything else in sight, and this couldn't be the only weapons cache—there must be more aircraft, other than the Adelpa 3 fighter jets Nev had seen with his own eyes—Enginsan was prepared for a war.

But with all of that armament at disposal, it also meant Nev had an even better chance of getting off planet.

The racked weapons were probably intended for the next phase, related to that lab, whatever it was in all of its evil incarnations, but Nev was going to use them for his own purposes.

Where initial missions seemed to have been about colonization, the next phase was meant to be the eradication of all indigenous wildlife deemed a threat by one deranged person before colonization could be attempted again.

The weapons hadn't been wielded outside the wire as far as he knew. They didn't look like they'd been fired since they'd been tested after manufacturing. They were too pristine.

Every weapon was oiled and shined as if meant to be hung on a wall like a trophy, not be wielded on the battlefield.

Noticing a console on the wall, he tapped it to bring up a digital map. No password was required. Apparently passwords weren't necessary here.

From the point of view of the current personnel, they were all on the same team, no doubt selected by Enginsan himself at this point—or selected by people he trusted—so there wouldn't be deepening levels of security in a traditional military sense.

But then why had Nev been taken? What was the true reason? Was it as simple as plain old revenge, and Enginsan arrogant enough to think that just a few mercs could dispose of him?

However many were involved, who he really was dealing with, all who were responsible, they definitely believed him to be dead, otherwise there would have been a search.

Currently Nev was invisible, and he couldn't wait to disappoint anyone involved in the plot to murder him.

Hopefully that would be by holding up his middle finger while flying away, but his inner soldier told him he would have to fight hard to get to that point in time.

Nev was fine with it. He hadn't participated in a battle in quite a while, had been essential during many battles, and in a strange way actually missed feeling integral to a mission. Because he was good at soldiering.

The current mission just happened to be one he'd planned himself.

According to the digital map, there were ammo boxes or weapon caches placed in equal intervals across the landscape—likely parachuted to the surface by aircraft—and they even looked to be worldwide.

He found himself hesitant to grab a weapon as he realized what was actually going on.

It finally sunk in that it was no longer about a colonization. He had no idea when or even if anyone would call this planet home.

And maybe not even consider it a vacation destination anymore either.

Before anything was imagined for the planet, if plans were named some other operation, or maybe not named at all, there would be an extermination. Who knew how long that would realistically take.

Once Enginsan was finished at the present location, he would likely expand across the planet. That was obvious. There were too many weapons and too many mercs.

And what they were all doing there was wrong.

I can't leave.

Not right away as he'd originally wanted to. Because he was already there. And also because of the weapon systems available. For him, that changed everything. The weapons meant leverage.

It was his chance to make up for all of the wrong he'd done during the initial phase of the mission before he'd escaped with Kate.

Or at least he'd try.

There was a huge difference between pulling the trigger to prevent an animal from attacking and hunting one down.

Nev searched for and found earplugs. He would need them considering what he would soon wield.

He would know more about Enginsan's plot in time. He could not and would not believe that anyone on this planet would join his side.

It was possible some of them were good people. But he didn't care. He couldn't allow himself to. They weren't military and they weren't following orders. They were lured by greed and were willing to wipe out other species in order to get rich.

Nev would consider every person he encountered to be his enemy until he returned to Kate.

LINK TO PRIMARY CACHE? LINK TO PLANETWIDE CACHES?

It was clear that the planet had been explored thoroughly since he'd set foot on it last. The attempts probably hadn't been accomplished entirely by humans though, but by data collecting probes.

The probe issue must have been solved. The one seen by them before the ride on the Cryton boat over to the complex when the flying creatures had attacked and destroyed them.

Nev guessed that there was some sort of shock device installed onboard a new version of the probes, similar to the shock prods they used aboard the Cryton boat on the way over to the complex to discourage the dog-sized water creatures.

His choice to remain and fight was the simplest choice he'd ever made in his life. It was his best chance to get back to Kate and also eliminate any threats who might come after him later.

Except, funnily enough, because he was human, he was starving. Fortunately, there weren't just weapons surrounding him, there were also plenty of MREs.

He ate one cold.

He hadn't touched explosives since he'd left the planet because he'd retired soon afterward, but he remembered how to use them.

The explosives he eyed were familiar. They mushed to almost any hard surface. He placed four, set the timers, and armed them with a flip of a switch.

It was time to get the battle started.

What would be his biggest threat, the mercs and all of the arsenal that Enginsan had supplied them?

Or the inhabitants with the keen sense of smell, powerful claws, razor sharp teeth, impressive speed, and visceral ability to hunt with stealth and had the most to lose?

Nev only had to think on it briefly.

CHAPTER 21

The explosion slowed all vehicular movement, rovers braking to a stop, but some sped away, necks craning. Even the mercs on foot twisted in the direction of the blast. Some were viewing with binoculars.

There were towers on base. Multiple Tactical Operation Centers maybe. Nev didn't know. If they were TOCs, Nev doubted they were being operated to military standard. They weren't an immediate threat to him.

His gut told him that there were few prior officers in merc uniforms, just grunts, so Nev's personal experience would keep him a step ahead of any immediate trouble for at least a while.

The erupting fireball had transformed into morphing smoke and caught the attention of the Adelpa 3s patrolling the airspace. Like starving predators on the hunt, they were Nev's immediate threat.

Their tight maneuvering capability allowed sharp turns to do a flyover and for the pilots to decide what the next plan of action would be, no doubt paying strict attention to radio chatter Nev was not privy to as they were emitted from the towers.

Holding a controller in each hand, a Devil hovering over one shoulder, and a Demon over the other, Nev was a one man army.

Especially considering each weapon system was now linked to the rest of Enginsan's uncountable ammo boxes.

Whenever it would be necessary, the Demon and Devil simply needed to be deployed for reloading. He would be smart enough only to send one weapon system at a time to dock on an ammo box to begin the bullet filtering process.

If millions of beasts hadn't killed him, and also some of the best trained soldiers in the universe, how would rusty mercs fare against him. Nev would definitely bet on himself under the unique battle conditions.

The only way to stop him was to pry the controllers from his dead hands and he didn't plan on dying until after he'd grown old with his wife.

Without waiting for any kind of aggression from the jets, and ignoring the part of him that thought that maybe he should consider rules of engagement, a part of him that was retired forever, Nev registered the targets in the digital sight lenses, tagging them.

Aiming, and after both weapon systems whined a simultaneous three-second delay, sounding like bombs that might explode, he squeezed the triggers on the controllers, firing the weapons over his shoulders.

Bright funnels of twenty-millimeter rounds arced into the sky, assaulting the airspace with surgical precision, bringing the nearest of the Adelpa 3 fighter jets crashing to the ground.

As the Adelpa 3 fighter jet was a fireball, the other Adelpa 3 targeted his area of operation, firing on him with its own chain guns, the pilot disregarding the danger he or she was putting fellow mercs in on the ground.

No doubt the pilot was alarmed and angry about what happened to the battle buddy who had just been flying the airspace, crashed, and was likely dead.

Likely thinking himself to be invincible, Nev hadn't seen the pilot hit the ejector seat in time.

Nev aimed at the other Adelpa 3. It nosed down on him, getting bigger every second, firing its weapons the entire way.

Nev held off on the Devil and pulled the trigger of the controller linked to the Demon, belching its four barrels of firepower.

Another of Enginsan's most destructive creations got brought down to the ground too. The Adelpa 3 was as much a smoky fireball as the other one, but it had hit closer to base. Closer than Nev had wanted.

The entire base was on alert. There were alarms and shouting and he was sure mercs were mobilizing to investigate what was happening or even start shooting.

But some of them must have been as confused as Nev hoped, the ones who hadn't noticed bullets arcing into the sky.

The mercs were ready for beasts to attack, so many of them must have believed there'd been an accident, or the beasts had somehow brought down the aircraft, which they were very capable of doing.

Maybe word of Nev being alive had reached the ears of higher, whoever higher really were, because who else would start attacking everyone, as he'd also prepared for the possibility of his anonymity vanishing.

But Nev couldn't risk being taken prisoner again. He'd survived multiple attempts on his life. It was only a matter of time until his luck ran out.

He'd lit the fuse of the battle, and war his way was the surest way for him to escape, and he had no reason to care about what happened to any of the people on Planet Adelpa.

The destruction caused by the exploding aircraft had greatly damaged the inner perimeter of the base on the far side and suddenly he felt like enemies were about to flood his position.

Nev's instincts always served him a little too well, in that he was often aware of a worst case scenario about to happen, and he was soon surrounded.

But not by who he expected.

CHAPTER 22

***They were hunting** me already.*

A Mauler, the close cousin to a Ravager, charged him with feline agility, tail thrashing back and forth, every muscular ounce of it telegraphing aggression. Nev had only a second to react. He nearly pulled a trigger.

But before Nev could make a move, or decide what to do about the rest of the Maulers, or the pack of Ravagers that appeared behind them, all of them as intent on tearing him apart with their own jaws and claws, the mother Ravager from the lab barked and loudly.

He recognized her, having been so close to her in the lab. They'd nearly been face to face when he'd unlocked the cage.

There were barks in response, and amazingly, the group of Maulers trotted forward and according to the way they'd positioned themselves, they'd been assigned for Nev's very own protection detail.

Nev breathed a sigh of relief, ignoring his flight response. The pup he'd shown care toward in the lab had a mother with power over others of her kind apparently, and also over Maulers.

Nev knew how smart they were. They'd seen Nev destroy the Adelpa 3s, a display of turning on his own species, and humans were the enemy of the Ravagers and the Maulers.

It was likely she'd escaped immediately, followed Nev, and waited to see what he would do.

None of the animals could know what he'd done in the past, it was all about the here and the now, but he would be wise to think of himself as only a temporary ally, for his own safety. He would not turn his back on any of the predators if he could help it.

The Ravagers immediately turned away from Nev and allowed him to pass as if he were suddenly invisible.

Along with Maulers, they must have been intent on freeing the Ravager in the lab, Nev realized, so it was fortunate he'd decided to be the one to let her out.

Even though he was armed, and could have fired on them, he had no idea how many predators surrounded the base. Out of sight for now.

The mother Ravager acknowledged Nev by snarling before leaving with her pup. If they met again, things might be different.

Message received.

The fierce killer that the Ravager was had been absent as it mothered the pup. Maybe the Ravager hadn't wanted to attack Nev in front of it.

Though it would be fiercer one day, the pup was young in mind, and its mother likely didn't want to show the pup that all humans were to be killed. It was a lesson, and that lesson had saved Nev's life.

He'd observed more of their behavior and now he had an even deeper understanding of their intelligence. It really made sense that the beasts were the dominant form of life on the planet.

Ravagers were probably smarter than even Nev understood, and he understood them to be highly intelligent, like humans, and had even witnessed that intelligence firsthand.

No doubt Maulers were just as intelligent as Ravagers, but still they followed commands by Ravagers.

The base continued to be a chaos, and no doubt mercs on the ground had glimpsed the beasts, because they were staying away.

No matter the reason the Maulers had been there originally, it had nothing to do with Nev. But everything had changed.

With the mother Ravager no longer in sight, as well as the squad of Ravagers there to help her escape, Nev was left to deal with the Maulers assigned to him.

Without the presence of the Ravagers, the apprehension between man and beast returned. Nev felt like an alien.

It was so awe inspiring to walk among such strength and savagery, something no human was supposed to do and live, or likely had ever done.

Maybe Nev did deserve to die for what he'd done. For how many of them he'd killed. He was about to find out.

No matter the command from the Ravager, the situation would be on his own terms.

He took his fingers off the triggers and raised the controllers, Demon and Devil aiming skyward.

The sudden movement spurred one of the Maulers to rush forward but then it halted its charge, just a threat, Nev hoped. He would know soon enough. He also hoped it could somehow understand.

"I'm not here to harm you. What humans are doing here is wrong. I just want to leave. But before I do, I'll help you do what needs to be done."

Although it seemed impossible for it to understand what he'd said, Nev speaking to it must have been comprehended as he'd intended because it dissolved the ferocious expression on its face.

Respect was very different than hate. And as much as he understood them, respect was likely a language that was universal. Him attempting to communicate was respectful.

Unblinking, the Mauler barked, and the Maulers surrounding it mimicked its vocalization, sounding to Nev like a version of a command. And that command was received and understood.

At least for now, they wouldn't harm him. What was happening was extraordinary. A short while ago, he'd been certain that he should trust no one else on the planet, but he'd never considered trusting beasts.

The situation would have been impossible during the mission, when he was an officer, and it likely would be impossible in the future because of the unique situation occurring at all.

But also, Nev wouldn't have encountered these specific Maulers. It would have been different ones, or just Ravagers. The trust that was currently happening was a rarity in the universe and across time.

A squad consisting of Maulers and a human would never happen again.

If the entire squad of Maulers protecting him died, he would be in as much danger as any of the other humans though. He needed to leave Planet Adelpa as soon as possible, or whatever this planet should actually be called.

Really, humans had no right to name it. It didn't belong to them. It belonged to the animals. So there shouldn't be a name, just those living here thinking of it as home.

The snub faced Maulers, sprouting large fangs downward from their mouths, all of their bodies striped, were pack hunters.

Temporarily, Nev was a member of that pack.

CHAPTER 23

All of their armament and weapons and vehicles, means to escape, were suddenly just stationary background. Symbols of human innovation but of no use to most of them. It was planned that way.

Watching them struggle to maintain their pride pleased Deviltooth as it dominated further onto stolen land. All land occupied by humans would soon be taken back and theirs once again.

A female Ravager and pup had been rescued. From where she'd been found, violence had been done to the dead before they'd died. The human inside, who was responsible, was killed. It was barked about.

There were no pups on the human base. There were no Mauler or Ravager females. And it seemed humans were turning on each other. They were free to maul and ravage as they pleased.

Voices caught its interest in its one good ear. Close by, hiding. The cowards should have been fighting. It found them quickly but remained unseen.

It watched as the two humans conversed without even knowing Deviltooth was there, allowing only its eyes to move back and forth, watching their conversation, deciding who was in charge.

It did not understand all of their language, only words that were said the most, like teeth, which humans feared greatly, or devil, named after the destructive human weapon during the battle when Deviltooth lost its fang.

A weapon they hoped would save them but had not because they'd had to leave.

Deviltooth understood tone very well, having spent many days out of sight of the first humans, listening and watching.

Both humans were frightened, defeated, even without entering the battle themselves. One was much taller and more muscular than the other one and for a moment, Deviltooth thought he was in charge.

But just as it had been for itself, size did not matter, and the taller human was more frightened than the shorter one who was attempting to calm him.

The shorter one was in charge because the human who was more impressive physically acted like an underling.

The language of the underling came out as pathetic gasps and the human in charge reached up and slapped him across the face, likely to motivate him.

That was a scenario it had experienced. Though smaller than most of its kind, its experience in battle made it much fiercer than others, its strategies much wiser too, even compared to Ravager General.

It heard enough, so it made its presence known, catching superior and underling by surprise, swiping twice, and both humans were on the ground, the taller falling as easily as the smaller, and both bleeding to death with shocked looks on their faces.

Neither of them had fired off a shot from the weapons they held. Quick barks signaled to its own underlings to drag away the bodies and quickly bury them and their weapons beneath the ground.

Fresh barks by it signaled others of its kind to hunt further into the temporary human territory.

A human threw down something they sometimes put in their mouths but did not eat, instead inhaling the smoke. The something was still smoking.

Did he not realize that it could start a fire? Fires made it possible to burn down entire forests.

Deviltooth had seen that happen before, and even before the humans landed. From lightning strikes.

And when the first it'd hunted, burned the grass on purpose. When it trapped them in the grass, and where one of them referred to it as armor that gallops.

It remembered the heat of the rushing flames, having nearly been burned were it not so agile.

Deviltooth allowed itself to be seen by the careless human who enjoyed smoke in his mouth.

Sensing shock was something it enjoyed the more it did it. The human must have sighted its eyes staring down at what still smoked.

Deviltooth wanted the human to know that it would be the one that would end his life but it didn't always need to attack.

A muffled bark commanded others waiting nearby, out of the human's view, for such a command.

The human was ravaged by Maulers from both sides before he could raise his communication device to his mouth.

Deviltooth left the area, but could still hear its underlings tearing the human apart, and his remains would soon be buried too.

It had commanded the attacks to happen before the humans could signal others of their kind, who were nearby. But it had wanted some communication to slip through. That was purposeful.

Fear about what was coming their way would be communicated to the rest with a panicked tone.

Fear could be as crippling as a severe wound.

CHAPTER 24

Well-armed mercs fought throughout the dirt streets of the base. The streets were probably supposed to have been paved already.

The hunters that existed on all fours had chosen to reveal themselves at the same time. As if they'd been commanded. So Nev gave himself permission to leave. They would accomplish what he wanted.

There were no longer any formations, no order, nothing that was reminiscent of what should happen under the circumstances; it was just human beings running for their lives in random directions or stopping to shoot.

Attacks lashed out in front of them no matter how quickly they fired their weapons, or how many grouped together, nearly all of them ended the same; with vicious swipes of clawed paws and gnashing teeth.

The results were dragged away screaming or unseen altogether; the echoes of their shouting and hollering, the last thing they could do to attempt to survive, was silenced forever.

Beasts evaded and dodged bullet fire as if they'd been trained to do so, which meant survivors of the mission had taught their offspring.

The outcome was men and women being ripped apart as if it were a competitive sport among the predators, and surely many of them were tasting human flesh for the first time. Often it was difficult to know if it was man or woman dying by the screaming.

Only the occasional grouping of people were able to kill one of the beasts, but comparatively there was no comparison, and soon afterward the victorious humans were ripped apart as well.

Nev was not so unlucky. Whenever a strange Ravager or Mauler approached, the lead Mauler barked, and then Nev could continue on. The Mauler squad continued to protect him.

As long as the Mauler squad lived, the Ravagers and the other Maulers wouldn't harm him.

But without them?

He couldn't allow his circumstances to be altered. He didn't want to find out. Not until he'd cleared the base.

Being so near them, he observed that many of them had scars. Scars meant they had fought one another for hierarchy, and the ones that battled for hierarchy but lost obeyed the victor. And Nev believed he had figured out their behavior even more.

The Maulers in the squad protecting him were as big and strong as any of the rest except there were hints of them being younger by the look in their eyes, reminding him of the innocence of the Ravager pup in the lab.

And it wasn't as if there hadn't been a power struggle between Maulers and Ravagers at some point during the planet's history. Nev suspected that it was going on even today.

How could it not?

Pushing back against leadership was natural for the young to do. It was something Nev remembered doing, having been a young soldier himself. But also being a former officer leading young soldiers.

There was always a span of time between when a new recruit was a blank slate to when they were indoctrinated into the beliefs of leadership.

Because of their intelligence, it seemed that the squad of Maulers were currently thinking for themselves. Maybe that was why they'd been chosen by the mother Ravager.

If they lived long enough to become leaders, Nev wondered if they would learn to trust humans. The thought almost made him feel sick, as angry as he'd felt when he'd encountered the doctor in the lab.

He wasn't sure how it would be possible, but he would do his best to dissuade them from trusting humans. Maybe he would shoot at them before he left. Shoot at them but not hit them. He hated the idea of doing that though. So far they were loyal.

Millions of beasts were incoming though, and he was certain none of *them* trusted humans. Nev had heard the report and many reports like it over the net like a squall out of nowhere, since the dead tended to drop radios.

Millions that didn't know Nev the same way as the Ravager he'd freed from the lab did, or the Mauler squad protecting him.

Tribes of individuals that could only assume Nev was like the rest of the humans on the planet and if they could, they would tear him to pieces, eat him, or bury whatever remained.

He'd never seen the burial behavior before, but because he'd never been in the situation, being protected by beasts, he was a silent observer. It was brilliant on their part.

Hiding the evidence of battle allowed the battle to continue. If ground was empty of carnage, it displayed the illusion of safety and they understood that.

Which was probably why the dead Ravager had been pulled out of the complex before him and his squad could finish their inspection during the mission ten years ago.

Another epic battle was on the horizon, maybe as hectic as that one had been, and it was likely there would be many more; Nev could sense it, but this was not his war.

No wars were, not anymore, and his life no longer belonged to only himself, it belonged to his wife, Kate. He must survive, fight like hell to protect himself in order to get back to her.

There was no way to communicate that to the impressive squad of Maulers guarding him. The curved, taut, and striped quadrupeds looked bulletproof.

Standing outdoors among the rest of the frantic humans was the best way to get slaughtered, no matter if he were guarded by the very beasts doing the slaughtering.

So, after some tense minutes while he deployed the weapons to be reloaded, under their protection, he ducked inside a large building that he hoped was a hangar. It was large enough to be.

Glancing behind him, the Maulers allowed it. They stood guard, and Nev wondered if they'd remain there.

CHAPTER 25

The well-lit expansion was empty aside from military grade cases that surely housed more weaponry and ammunition. The familiar cases gleamed with shiny new unused, but them being unopened was probably meant only to be temporary.

That had been the plan until the war started outside the walls without warning. Nev could have asked the lone man facing him —as if he'd been expecting him—but he sensed he wouldn't get an honest answer.

Although he wasn't armed, he seemed a worthy threat, and Nev had reloaded the weapons just in time.

Devil and Demon hovered over either shoulder. One squeeze of either trigger from either controller and the man would be red paste.

"Quite the place to hide, eh."

Both of Nev's trigger fingers rested on the triggers. "So, that's what you've been doing."

"Negative. Been hunting you. Had you in my sights. But I didn't shoot."

"Obviously." Nev was unnerved but he refused to allow anyone to have dominion over him. "Then you understand what I'm capable of."

"I let the leash out but I've reeled you back in. I know you're trying to get out of here but that isn't going to happen."

"Is that a fact."

"I would do the same if I were you."

"And how is it you're going to stop me?"

"I've always been skilled at hunting. All of my strengths branch from it. It's my mission to keep you here and ensure that you die for what you've done."

Although the stranger was intimidating, Nev likely had faced tougher before, and even fought them hand to hand, as he did with Major Makada, or Nimbus.

Nev remembered the skiff mission, how there was no airspace coordination area established and he'd faced uncountable numbers of the beasts while armed with Shoulder Devils, and he'd survived that too.

He hadn't lived through everything that happened on this planet only to die now, not be killed by some stranger with a threatening demeanor.

What was strange was that the stranger wasn't intimidated by the weapons Nev wielded.

"Who the hell are you, and why the hell do you care whether I live or die?"

He smirked. "You're the one who killed Ryke."

Nev decided to play his game. "How did you really find me?"

"I bugged the skiff. I thought you might get out of there."

"Some hunter."

"Yet here we are."

He was beginning to look more and more familiar. As if Nev had met him before. Except he knew he hadn't. He would have remembered. Which meant he was related to someone he knew.

No, that wasn't it, he didn't know him. He'd never met him. But he must be related to him. He had to be his grandson.

Nev had seen pictures of Corbin Mero before. In those pictures, he was always dressed in a suit and a tie with a friendly toothless smile that contrasted someone who was capable of creating weapons of the most sinister kind like Mero gas.

"Corbin Mero . . . the third? You exemplify all the characteristics of descendants who inherit as opposed to have to work for it."

"Exemplify. Hmm."

Corbin Mero's grandson had an unkempt beard, and his confidence faltered. The jab wounded his ego. Maybe even more than the bullets Nev wanted to shoot at him to get him out of the way.

Nev decided to use his knowledge against him. Mero knew the

truth anyway.

"Don't forget Kilroy, but Ryke was that coward picking off Ravagers with that sniper rifle of his. Everyone on that A-brid died the moment they decided to involve themselves in my attempted murder. If they weren't dead after I shot them, then they burned to death after the A-brid crashed. Ryke must have been your friend. The hell with him."

Mero was angry. "Yeah, he was my friend. I'm here to finish the job. Hunting down vermin is what I've always done well. The status of your life is contingent on my deal, so your death is a foregone conclusion."

Nev didn't react. "With everything going on outside, good luck getting whatever payment you're after."

Before recent events, for Nev, most of the fistfights he'd gotten himself into were linked to a military mind frame, but now he was a civilian, so he was done throwing fists. Ryke and his fellow merc had been the final exception, hopefully for the rest of his life.

And he no longer had the patience for any rules of engagement. Nev aimed Devil and Demon, painted a target stripe over Mero, and pulled the triggers.

Nothing happened. There wasn't even a three-second delay from either weapon.

Mero grinned and raised some sort of device. Something small that had been hidden in the palm of his hand and had obviously interfered with the lasso communication between controllers and weapons.

"Shit."

Nev threw down the controllers, sensing the Devil and Demon remaining where they were, and charged Mero.

So much for not throwing fists anymore.

Mero smiled, showing small, gapped teeth, and raising fists. It seemed that was exactly what he wanted to happen, so Nev wouldn't disappoint him.

When Nev got close enough, he lunged at Mero's waist, but Mero sprawled hooking under his arms, and Nev instantly felt an elbow raining down against his back over and over, taking the breath out of him.

Then a bicep looped under Nev's armpit and he was flipped onto his back. Mero was on top of him immediately, hands crossed, each fist with a fistful of collar, and then he twisted his fists.

Staring up at the man trained well in hand to hand combat, especially on the ground, Nev saw stars zipping by as the pressure from Mero's knuckles pushed into the sides of his neck.

A buzzing sound filtered into his hearing and grew louder and louder.

Mero wasn't just trying to make him unconscious, Nev knew. He'd said it. He meant to kill him.

Though he was outmatched physically, and probably training, Nev had a lot more experience in hand to hand combat than Mero did because he was older.

But not just winning a fight. Getting his ass kicked.

So Nev did to Mero what a fellow soldier attempted to do to Nev at a bar when he was fresh out of basic training. Except Nev couldn't miss. His life depended on it.

With both hands, Nev transformed his fingers into bowl shapes tight enough to scoop and hold water.

And with all of his strength—knowing what it meant, understanding that if he didn't hit him with every bit of strength he had, feeling unconsciousness seeping in and warming every bit of him—he grunted and clapped both hands against the sides of Mero's shaved head.

Mero's grip relented immediately with ruptured eardrums in both ears. His equilibrium off, it probably felt to him like he might be the one looking up, not down.

Nev shuffled himself out from under Mero on his shoulder blades, using them like feet, and kicked out with a boot when Mero reached for his left one, snapping his jaw to the side.

Another debilitating wound.

Nev scrambled to his feet and ran for the nearest case and threw it open. Inside was not the weapon he expected. There was no time for the part of him that marveled at modern weaponry.

He'd never fired it, or even seen it fire in person, but he'd heard about it and seen the schematics.

He was thankful he was so proficient at analyzing multiple weapon systems, even ones he never anticipated wielding, especially after retiring.

Inside the case was the M112a2 weapon system.

After the blows to the back and nearly having his windpipe crushed, Nev was definitely done using his fists to get himself out of situations. Not once he was armed again.

Instead of forcing a reboot and reestablishing connections between controllers and Demon and Devil—there wasn't enough time—he remembered he had multi-linked every cache.

Multi-link meant a universal trigger. He grabbed one controller and linked it to the M112a2. Too fast for Mero to sever the fresh link, which required two registered sources, which also required more than just a few seconds.

But Mero obviously didn't know that.

Mero looked shocked when the M112a2—a.k.a. the Shoulder Dragon—rose up over Nev's shoulder, Dragon Scale tilted down.

Mero's confidence vanished.

Nev pulled the trigger of the controller, feeling the heat even above the Dragon Scale as the Shoulder Dragon's orange-blue flame stretched out as a cone shaped sun, illuminating the darkness.

Mero kept presenting the device that had hobbled the firing capability of the Shoulder Devil and Shoulder Demon, his eyes huge, squeezing the button over and over in a panic, even as he was engulfed.

"NOOOOO-AHHHHH!"

Mero's screaming evaporated as his flesh melted off his bones and his skeleton was revealed and buckled.

CHAPTER 26

The Shoulder Dragon shot a flame that could burn through a wall made of steel at thirty meters.

The differentiating aspect of the M112a2 compared to the M112a1 was that the M112a2 didn't require a refill. Its reproduction began every time the trigger was squeezed.

Though the firer must pause every thirty seconds so that the barrel didn't begin to malform or eventually melt away, beneath the barrel was a heat shield nicknamed the Dragon Scale.

An accurate weapon, but the firer always needed to remain cautious and maintain awareness of where what was being fired at ignited. Dragons could easily melt the floor being stood upon.

Ground forces had been intended to deploy where air power could not reach. The M112a2s had been shipped as a last ditch effort for ground forces to complete any extermination missions artillery failed to.

Enginsan had his genetic samples and secreted away his plans for whatever he wanted to do with them, but he smartly anticipated survivors.

Regardless, the Shoulder Dragons, the most impressive flame throwers ever created, were intended to burn anything that got in the way of the man at the top.

Had Enginsan forgotten about what happened to Colonel Pritchard's battalion? Nev had not. Then again Enginsan likely didn't care. People were expendable to him as long as he got what he wanted, which was another planet to play with.

An aircraft was incoming. He heard it before he looked up, spotting the unmistakable dark triangle against a blue sky. He painted a target over the incoming Adelpa 3.

The aircraft was likely assigned to Mero, and it seemed the pilot had cleared the immediate area of threats, allowing Nev time to think, but it was clear what the command was if Nev were the one to emerge and not Mero.

Because there were Shoulder Dragons, there were endless cases filled with Dragon Scales. The Scales weren't only heat shields for the Dragons, but they were also bulletproof, and they could be controlled too.

Nev used the thumb lever on the side of the controller to activate hundreds of the magnetized bulletproof Scales and link them to the controller controlling the Shoulder Dragon.

Now he was armed with a Shoulder Demon, a Shoulder Dragon, and as many Dragon Scales that he could control.

He'd practiced using the Scales in a simulator before retiring to the point when he wasn't just good at making shapes, it was fun. The Scales could move as quickly as the fingers.

And the controller linked to the Scales reacted to whichever fingers formed shapes. Using his thumb, he formed them as a dome, layering them on top of one another like a shell, just as the Adelpa 3 fired on his location.

Bullets ricocheted off the impenetrable defense he'd created.

Using the Demon, and as he'd already targeted the Adelpa 3, he simply pressed the autofire button on the controller in there with him, blindly shooting from beneath his bulletproof protection.

He couldn't see its destruction but he heard it, and felt the vibration of the crash, which allowed him the temporary safety to form a window through the Scales.

As far as he could tell, there were no more Adelpa 3s in the airspace.

The rest of the humans were not doing so well. He caught glimpses of them being stalked and killed and slaughtered in the distance, and their remains were being fought over.

A Ravager stalked someone from behind, so quietly and lunging so quickly, it was as if it was floating like one of the weapon systems Nev wielded.

It rose into view of a merc, showing itself and all of its strength and ferocity, before snarling, but a different Ravager took the merc down. Then both Ravagers fought over the kill.

There was nothing Nev could do to prevent what was happening. And he had been noticed too, by a scarred Mauler missing an ear, menacing at the front of a squad of Ravagers.

Nev wanted to attempt the same thing he'd done to win over the Mauler squad to the new Mauler, who seemed to be in charge.

But he hesitated.

Because of where it positioned itself, it was clearly respected by Maulers and Ravagers alike. And then something peculiar happened.

The Mauler vocalized a strange bark, one Nev had heard before, and it sounded like information and a command at the same time.

Ravagers growled a new bark with consistency. Nev counted. It was like a cadence. The Mauler had communicated something to the rest of them and they'd reacted, as if they all hated him at once.

It made Nev feel similarly to the moment he strode into the TOC to confront Horne during the mission. He hadn't been a traitor, but he was viewed as one, and that was how he felt now. Also, and also strange, was that somehow he'd been recognized.

The Mauler before him was very different than the others. Like certain Ravagers Nev encountered during the skiff mission, it too emanated power.

And he couldn't be sure, but it looked like there was recognition in the eyes of the Mauler whose front fang was missing.

It sneered then, almost a smile, something Nev would never forget; an imitation of its superior when Nev faced it before leaving the planet.

A taunt.

"Holy . . ."

The Mauler had been among the millions he'd fought while aboard the skiff mission during Operation Tuhrelevim. How else could it recognize him, and to sneer, knowing what it meant.

The tip of a spear comprised of Maulers as well as Ravagers, Nev was staring at the new leader of the beasts on this planet. He was certain. And it behaved as though Nev understood what it was, and what it represented.

He didn't know what to do next. There were thousands of beasts in and around the base but he knew how many there actually were.

There were 40,000 rounds in the Demon. And the flame of the Dragon only reached so far.

CHAPTER 27

What Nev wasn't expecting was that the Mauler squad that protected him to reappear—they'd survived the last Adelpa 3 he'd shot down—understanding the danger Nev was in, and charged the newcomers.

Weapons hovering over his shoulders, Nev thought quickly, and Dragon Scales became a bridge of magnetically linked platforms in the air as predatory shapes darted beneath him. He nearly fell off.

Behind him was as loud of a dogfight he'd ever heard. He turned briefly. The clawing and biting was a blur, and bloody wounds appeared out of nowhere.

Growling snarls, yelps of pain, anger, defeat, victory, it all happened so fast.

But there were victors even faster, because the Mauler squad protecting Nev had been young and inexperienced, and they hardly lasted against the Mauler leader.

The Mauler, followed by Ravagers and Maulers it commanded, had won the fight and were coming for Nev as he stepped off the Scale running. He knew that without looking again because there was a roar chorus.

Nev had heard the vocalizations before, during the mission. It reminded him of right after radio silence or whispered orders between soldiers before an open command to attack.

Confidence emanated in waves, and they were speaking, communicating, talking to one another openly in their language of roars and growling and barks. Or more accurately, a back and forth communication of barks and roars only they understood.

Multiple voices and then thousands more. Commands and acknowledgement. Directives were not only being given but also understood.

Nev got the feeling it meant that they believed themselves to be winning the war.

The victorious celebrating was deafening, and Nev didn't doubt their forthcoming victory for a second. He had ears and eyes and he had to get out of there now.

All of them seemed to go after him at once, as if he were the last remaining human alive on the planet, or the last one who they cared about.

It was probably because they'd been ordered to. Most of the humans were running for their lives, and some were even running for their lives outside base, as all paths to vehicles were blocked.

Beasts killed anyone who got close.

The exception were the few A-brids that were airborne in helicopter formation, the gyrations of the blades of the hybrid jet/helicopters looking like insects fluttering the sky.

Who knew how far the pilots would fly them. As far and as long as the fuel lasted, probably.

But there were Ravagers and Maulers stalking them.

Sensing the incoming threat of teeth and claws, too fast for him to build a bridge, once again Nev formed the dome of Scales.

Because he had to keep a slit of a window, he constantly shifted where the dome protected, and the beasts started jumping onto the dome itself.

The weight of them bowed the Scales at the window, and claws clipped his right shoulder.

He yelled and there was snarling.

He was bleeding but the attack could have been worse. He moved his arm around. It was a bloody wound he could handle and also his hand moved well enough to handle the controller, but another breach and he'd be torn apart.

Thinking quickly, using his thumb in rapid swiping motions, he was able to form the dome so that it covered him completely and he brought it down into the dirt.

Obscured protection from within meant he couldn't shoot with a clear view because he couldn't see, and he couldn't remain there forever.

Sensing where they'd grouped, and understanding the behavior of predators all too well, he took his greatest risk yet, and briefly fanned open the Scales in the shape of a door.

Displaying the open vulnerability of his back.

CHAPTER 28

Nev felt the shift of their weight through the ground like a thousand horses galloping at once and quickly, he formed the Scales solid, and the beasts rammed the Scales where his back had just shown.

Identifying their position, and with stragglers in sight through a newly formed window, Nev fired Demon and Dragon.

Bullets crippled the momentum of the fast moving quadrupeds, chewing through their legs and bodies and heads, and fire from the Dragon burned any of them that got close to the dome.

Nev hoped that it would be the final battle between the beasts and himself, the one man army that he was.

He caught glimpses of that Mauler running the perimeter, a blur behind those protecting him, and they were dying for his cause.

Outside the impenetrable dome was a storm of growls and snarls, endless attacks and frustration as every one of them wanted to chew off a piece of the armor and sink their teeth into him.

With the dome almost entirely closed off, and knowing where most of the enemy stood their ground, and knowing there would be no humans to harm, Nev blind-fired the Demon, allowing the Dragon to cool.

The Demon fired hundreds of rounds from its four barrels. Nev was protected within the dome; it was similar to commanding artillery strikes from the safety of a TOC.

Angry and frustrated snarls, powerful animals whimpering in the throes of death, but then silence. As if all of them had disappeared.

The storm of snarling lifted and vanished.

But then there were barks.

Commands but it wasn't by a Ravager. It was by that Mauler. The one that led them. The one with all of the power.

Suddenly claws appeared upside down against the flat of the dirt to his left, nearly an entire paw appearing within the dome itself as it yanked upward, grasping hold of a Scale at the bottom of the defense Nev built.

Then it happened again near the same spot, and daylight intruded as cloudy beams, and there was more and more light with every Scale stolen away.

Deviltooth's plan was working. It saw glimpses of the human that shot it long ago, destroying its front fang.

Drooling, it wanted to kill him more than anything else during its life.

More than Mauler Commander before it.

And even more than Ravager General that had led them all.

It was facing the most powerful of the humans.

Those Deviltooth commanded understood their objective; rip away his defenses piece by piece.

Deviltooth tongued its sore fang and anticipated its next—but most satisfying—human kill.

More and more paws appeared and yanked upward, grabbing Scales away. Scales were bulletproof, and together they could form practically impenetrable shapes, but each of them only weighed a few pounds.

Far less than a one-ton Ravager or even Maulers with all of their wild strength and agility.

Scales kept disappearing, so many that it was apparent the beasts were transferring the Scales from paws to maws. Nev saw it happening.

Taking the Scales out of the fight, they struggled with them like caught fish as the magnetic control over them by the controllers

Nev held, did not subside.

That Mauler torpedoed into the opening, catching its head enough to slow it, and Nev lifted a leg as jaws bit but missed, its tail flipping.

A jagged tooth looked raw and sore, its angry eyes reflecting in the darkness of the dome, glowing, its growling magnified within such a small space, and Nev felt slobber drench his leg like warm rain.

Within a fraction of a second, Nev flung his thumb and flipped scales against him like a slap, just as he made another vicious lunge, shoving the Mauler away long enough for Nev to seal his protection.

The creature in charge showed again in the distance, standing menacingly on four powerful legs, facing Nev. It was out of breath and where once he saw confidence on its face, now Nev sensed frustration.

Nev aimed and fired at the ranks protecting him, decimating their defenses, dropping creatures right and left, and just as the Mauler in charge realized the danger he was in, and galloped around, it was too late.

The fire of the Dragon was inescapable aimed ahead of his path and where Nev anticipated he would go.

The Mauler tumbled as flame and his death caused an uproar. He had more power over the rest of the animals than Nev had realized, giving him the time to open the dome.

They, like human soldiers, seemed to follow orders, and seemed confused about what to do next.

CHAPTER 29

With the rest of the universe embracing modern day technology, Enginsan—and the military while Nev served—embraced the old, namely fuel.

The power was like an ancient tomb that was long buried but pried open greedily by a man so determined, all the while understanding that the tracking signatures of what everyone else was using for power was well documented.

What had been used to drive vehicles on Earth would not show up easily for anyone watching the universal radar, and although an expensive transportation and dangerous for the transporters, what did that matter to a man as rich and reckless as Enginsan Adelpa.

Almost every tool in Enginsan's arsenal was invisible because almost all of it could be burned. That was risky but purposeful.

What a great idea.

Spying the giant drum shapes he recognized as a fuel depot in the distance, he targeted it with the Demon and pulled the trigger.

The Shoulder Demon rose up to the appropriate height, angled so subtly it could hardly be seen, and fired when Nev pulled the trigger of the controller.

Drums turned into fireballs in the distance about a second before the explosions were heard. The ground shook beneath his feet, causing the distraction he'd intended. But the eruptions still didn't deter them all.

The Scales were an extension of his will, so instead of a bridge, this time he formed them as a staircase, one that he could barely keep footing on as he had to leap up the ascendance of jaws gnashing beneath and his balance was lacking.

Ravagers leapt onto backs, building a ladder. A fourth, then a fifth tall. The sixth scrambled up the ladder of striped legs but the weight of them was too much and all of them leaned, collapsed, and fell over.

They were back on their clawed paws and determined to discover a better way to get at him in an instant.

Nev exhaled, having to concentrate on what needed to be done next, when he heard a roar of victory, chilling his blood.

Glancing, a Mauler pulled itself up onto a Scale. Maybe it had leapt from one of the nearby buildings. It balanced awkwardly, leaning forward and backward, growling at him.

But Nev selected and dropped the Scale beneath it, and it fell with a jarring impact when it hit the ground, but it didn't kill it.

Others had the same idea, launching from anything higher than the ground, most missing, some touching the bottom of a Scale, and then a Ravager held onto one and climbed itself up.

Because of the link, Nev could control any Scale he wanted, which included the ones that had been stolen away from the dome. He simply moved whichever one was closest since the technology was based on proximity.

Nev had no choice but to drop all of the Scales behind him—there was no going back now—and could use them later.

He continued to build the staircase higher and higher away from the threats beneath, ignoring their threatful roaring.

From this point on, it was all about going forward.

The unrelenting retaliation grew more disturbing. Especially when Ravagers attacked ammo boxes in the distance. They understood that the functionality of at least one of the weapons he wielded were linked to them having watched it reload.

But Nev lured many of them away and was able to circle back and make it to an Adelpa Rover—Mero's ID card was clipped to the rearview mirror—and he had driven a good distance from base.

He considered using a mine layer, shooting the disk-shaped motion sensing weapons that would explode on impact, placing them strategically along his path to help protect himself, but he would only kill them if he had to.

Since the mission, he had accepted how intelligent the animals of the planet were, and he no longer needed to degrade them in his mind in order to combat them. Using a mine layer might accidentally kill beasts after he'd left the planet, which would be wrong.

He was done with wrong. His objective was to evade and escape.

He had done quietly as a soldier. He could do it as a former one too, so instead of laying mines, which would have been more effective, when he had to, he would loft stun grenades at any beasts that got too close.

Once clear of any threats, he drove back around but in a very wide circle, steering away whenever necessary. Thankfully the mercs had drawn away many of the beasts too.

But they would no doubt return to scour every inch of the base in time, to finish off any remaining humans, or ensure that there were no more of them living before hunting down stragglers.

Mercs could be seen in the distance still fighting, wielding the weapons Nev had used, Shoulder Devils, but they weren't nearly as effective with them and were taken down one by one, the arcs of bullets falling away like snuffed out flames.

CHAPTER 30

Enginsan was surely paying attention to how wrong things were going for him on the planet, but from orbit. There was no way he would lower himself to be on the surface.

Nev attempted contact through a vehicular channel on the console and waited. Enginsan eventually appeared onscreen and recognized Nev, but looked like he'd been expecting someone else.

Nev glanced down at the screen as he drove. "How many Adelpa one transport ships are incoming?"

Enginsan's perturbed expression was leaned into by someone briefly but a whisper sent him away.

"Do I need to repeat myself?"

"None at the moment."

"How many are scheduled? How many people have agreed to come here?"

"I assume you have a point."

"Turn them away. You've lost. And will lose everything."

"We'll see."

"*Seeing* is what I do best because I'm on the ground, not hiding in space like a fucking coward."

Enginsan's lips pursed. "Where are you?"

"So I can be targeted? I don't think so. You've already murdered too many people."

"I did nothing of the sort."

"You sealed their fates the moment you sent them here. And that's not counting how many thorns in your side who've conveniently disappeared here."

"One more would be nice."

"Not even you can sweep such crimes under the rug this time."

"You must believe you're going to survive. And leaving."

"I will."

"What do you want? To gloat?"

It was an obvious question but Nev asked anyway. "Why was I targeted by your mercenaries?"

Enginsan hesitated. He wasn't used to backing down from anyone, and he casually sipped from a white coffee mug with his brand emblazoned in blue. He sensed Enginsan was about to end the communication.

Nev had no doubt that Enginsan had been questioned before, and he'd likely told whoever was asking what they wanted to hear, but then had them killed and covered it up later. He would talk.

"I know what was going on in the lab."

Enginsan's eyes widened and he looked away, squinting briefly.

"Tell me why I was targeted by your mercs."

"You were a witness."

"I wasn't the only one."

"But one of the survivors. I suppose I should start at the beginning. I owe you that much I'm afraid. And even though we have a sordid past, I do respect you. Even more so now."

Nev saw through Enginsan's bullshit. He didn't care about his feigned respect, and pretended to ignore his quick glances away from the monitor and brief nods, surely alerting underlings to locate Nev's position so he could be fired upon.

Then this communication, any record of Enginsan incriminating himself, would be discovered and deleted.

But for Nev, it was worth the risk. "I'm listening."

"The first encounter with them was a shameful one. The explorers encountered their pups initially, essentially. Half grown, the pups were misidentified as a threat and the explorers felt they had no choice but to defend themselves. Unbeknownst to them, they didn't realize they were the young of the very large adults."

"Humans started the Ravager War?"

"The adult creatures had never encountered humans, so they'd allowed their pups to roam territory they controlled and dominated long ago."

"But even with the danger at a certain point, you decided to keep the momentum going."

"Failure is always the beginning. Success often inevitable. And worthy of any speed bumps."

"Speed bumps, huh?"

"Precisely."

"For you. Not for those who lost their lives."

"Speak to their families about that. They were compensated and generously."

"That's the problem. To people like you, it always comes down to money."

"Everything does."

"If the military couldn't give you what you wanted, you think mercenaries can?"

Enginsan only stared.

"How old are you?"

"None of your business."

"You look quite young for how old I suspect you are, yet you make decisions as if you'll live forever. You're choosing your pride over a planet and all of its life. Considering no one lives forever, decisions that profit you are ones that only give you the illusion of control—"

"Your opinion."

"And only temporarily. Most people live less than a hundred years. Why disrupt something that's existed for millions? It's a crime others will have to pay for. The consequences of your actions will echo long after you're gone."

"What business is it of yours, *Captain*?"

"I'm not in the military anymore."

"We all make decisions that have consequences."

Nev stomped on the brake, sliding toward a boulder but stopping the vehicle just in time. He put it in reverse and steered back onto the flat, checking his mirrors for any threats.

When Nev looked at the monitor again, Enginsan was smirking. "Tuhrelevim. What does that even mean? Did you name it?"

"Turner, Ulbright, Hall, Rogers, Evans, Lee, Ellis, Verano, Illingsworth, and Moore, the initial of the last name of every major investor."

"I didn't hear your name or Horne's. I thought it was Horne who had the most influence, but it was you all along. From the beginning. Horne was just a grunt."

"Everyone is a grunt to me."

"We grunts get the real work done. Why just those names?"

"Their egos. But there were many silent investors."

"I wonder why. Which of them did you murder? Correction, did you have murdered. I'm sure you weren't man enough to do it yourself."

Enginsan smiled. "Why bother asking when you know the answer."

"You made the mistake of involving me. Taking me away from my wife. Jeopardizing my life and causing the chance of making her a widow. That's unacceptable. You're going to pay for even considering it."

"Amusing."

CHAPTER 31

Nev's repeated attempts to contact Enginsan again eventually worked, and not just based on what Nev had explained to his underlings to annoy him to the point for at least one more communication.

There was an alarm sounding where Enginsan was located, and accompanying panic on his face as well. "What have you done?"

"You are a civilian with no military training. You think that throwing mercs and firepower at a planet will make you the owner of it. That couldn't be farther from the truth. Ignorance of the inhabitants only meant dooming more humans. Because of your mistakes, I can beat you no matter how many weapons you have."

"What have you *done*?!"

Not all of the Adelpa 3 fighter jets had been destroyed. The controls were straight forward. That was especially obvious after skimming the field manual in the cockpit, but the cockpit was different than the first he'd ever seen, schematically.

Nev had flown on Adelpa aircraft, but never an Adelpa 3, and this one—and the ones he'd shot down—was the newest version. It had been changed, upgraded, and probably all of them had been also.

Judging the simplistic design, the upgrades had happened multiple times, maybe even a few times a year since Nev had retired. It was as if Enginsan imagined piloting the aircraft and strafing the planet himself.

And for that to be possible, everything needed to be dumbed down, which was perfect for Nev. He didn't mind a cockpit that could be jumped into and flown as easily as driving a rover at all.

Similar to an A-brid, how Adelpa HJCs could transform from a jet to a helicopter; with the push of a few buttons, the capability of the Adelpa 3 fighter jet could transform as well. But they could fly in space.

That was probably why he hadn't seen the Adelpa 3s carving through the sky right away, they'd been in orbit. And that was the main reason Nev altered his plan.

If he'd somehow gotten a hold of Enginsan, kicked his ass like he deserved, and dumped him on the surface like it had been done —to Nev and countless others—his gut told him Enginsan would somehow survive.

Surely there were contingency plans. Only a fool would get this far into deep water and not know how to swim. Either Enginsan would be rescued or he had a backup plan if he ended up being stranded.

Most rich people were quite brilliant. Nev never doubted Enginsan's intelligence, which was why he needed to destroy the foundation of the problem.

The distance and coordinates were shown on the display in large green numbers against a dark background.

Enginsan was pure civilian, so much so that it was obvious he envied true soldiers like Nev had been. The danger of civilian designs was mostly accessibility. All one needed to do was press a button most of the time.

Nev understood Enginsan to be an egomaniac and would have bet he didn't only imagine himself firing the weapons he'd helped design but also being a regular pilot, maybe even flying an Adelpa 4 transport ship seated with select elite to stroke his ego as they thanked him.

Civilian designed weaponry and also aircraft.

After further examination, it had been obvious that the Adelpa 3 jet also had an autopilot capability.

But even if things went sideways, he probably could have figured out how to pilot the aircraft himself because of so many repetitions of having to figure out a backup plan when the first plan went wrong.

And a destination afterward wouldn't be a problem. The space station Enginsan was located on wasn't the only one.

Whenever a planet was colonized, there were a trail of them, like a long segmented bridge leading out into space. Docking on any of them may prove dangerous, but one step at a time.

Nev considered firing on the planet to destroy the leftover weapons, but he didn't want to kill any more of its rightful inhabitants by causing more explosions, and he was willing to allow the people down there to continue fighting for their lives.

Not that there was much hope for them, but he wouldn't interfere either way. He didn't want to kill them either.

From the cockpit, and using what was meant for destroying life on the planet, Nev launched a missile at Enginsan's command station in space, what surely housed mysteries and contingencies to keep the egomaniac and his many plans going.

There was a flash of light, and everyone involved in those plans were killed by the blast or were sucked out into space.

Enginsan had believed that he could remove himself from danger but he'd been wrong.

Setting recognizable coordinates, Nev accelerated further away from a planet that would exist only in his memory.

Soon, there were only stars and the cold darkness of empty space, until eventually a landing destination appeared. He had two Rovla assault rifles alongside him. Both were loaded and he had extra loaded magazines.

Nev had allowed the planet's rightful inhabitants to have their territory back. Under their control was how it should be.

Nev's role in the Ravager War was finally over. But if anyone decided to replace Enginsan Adelpa and take over his role, there might be some side missions.

Nev had done quietly before and would do it again if it were necessary. Hopefully, it wouldn't be.

Hopefully the first recognizable face would be happy to see him and call him Rob. Except Kate would probably call him Robert

Henry Nev. Rob would deserve that, but he would explain what happened.

www.ingramcontent.com/pod-product-compliance
Lightning Source LLC
LaVergne TN
LVHW050557160826
845677LV00011B/2351

9798840865729